CRESCENT EARTH

CRESCENT EARTH

BOOK 1

To Nikki,

Thank you for your support and positive energy!

Happy reading!

Ilia Epifanov

ILIA EPIFANOV

NEW DEGREE PRESS

CRESCENT EARTH

Book 1

ISBN   978-1-63676-499-3 *Paperback*

           978-1-63730-465-5 *Kindle Ebook*

           978-1-63730-466-2 *Ebook*

For those I love.

CONTENTS

CHAPTER 1 9

CHAPTER 2 21

CHAPTER 3 37

CHAPTER 4 45

CHAPTER 5 55

CHAPTER 6 61

CHAPTER 7 69

CHAPTER 8 79

CHAPTER 9 89

CHAPTER 10 97

CHAPTER 11 107

CHAPTER 12 113

CHAPTER 13 121

CHAPTER 14 129

CHAPTER 15 141

CHAPTER 16 147

CHAPTER 17 157

CHAPTER 18 163

CHAPTER 19 171

CHAPTER 20 179

CHAPTER 21 189

CHAPTER 22 199

CHAPTER 23 207

CHAPTER 24 217

CHAPTER 25 225

CHAPTER 26 233

ACKNOWLEDGMENTS 237

CHAPTER 1

———

There isn't much to say about the diner. It takes up the first floor of a two-story building, and its large rectangular windows offer a look into a different, though some might say *better*, time a couple centuries back. Not that anyone truly remembers. I grab a table and hang my coat and hat on a wooden rack and slide into a cracked vinyl booth.

"Dr. Williams!" the waitress calls. Her name is Kris, and she wears black slacks and a silky white shirt with no collar. "The usual?"

I nod with a small smile Kris is used to, and she hurries away without conversation. Moments later, she returns with a pot of coffee and a mug. "Enjoy!"

I do as I watch the night outside beyond a curtain of drizzle. My date arrives sometime later, and when I turn to see her walk in, I have to brace myself for a long moment. She is just as I remember her, except not at all. Nineteen now. All grown up. She waves and smiles when she sees me. I return the gestures and stand up to greet her. A few inches taller than me, she wears a buttoned-up black shirt dress that ends just below her knees and black laceless tennis shoes with red holographic animals dancing on the vamps. She takes off her black hat, revealing a buzz cut.

"Carmen," I say. "I'm glad you could make it."

"Of course," she says, and she offers her hand. "It's been a minute, huh?"

It's a little awkward, neither of us sure how to proceed. The instinct tells me to embrace her, but I simply shake her hand and invite her to sit down. "It's been more than that," I say. Almost a decade, in fact. "Coffee?"

Kris sets another mug on the table, and Carmen asks for a light dinner.

"Dr. Williams," she says when Kris is gone, "thank you for giving me this opportunity. I'm . . ." She laughs nervously. "This is so awkward."

"A little bit, isn't it?" I nod understanding. "How is your mother?"

Carmen sighs, and I almost regret mentioning the only thing we have in common. "Same old *mama*, always busy, always working. She oversaw my training until I enlisted, which—huge surprise!—she wasn't a fan of. She wants me to stay in the family biz."

"Have you told her about your promotion yet?"

"I haven't," she replies with a shrug, "but she knows. She always knows, doesn't she?"

"She has always known," I agree.

Kris brings her food, and I keep drinking coffee. Carmen pokes at her salad with a fork, and then looks up at me. "I'm not going to call you Dad."

I utter a laugh and marvel at her. I say, "No, of course not, Carmen. I wouldn't expect you to."

She breathes out. "Good." The pause lingers. We don't have much to discuss, despite the years apart. She chews on a leaf of red cabbage and says, "Now, I've been briefed about tonight's mission, but I still don't understand what it entails."

"I'll say more on our way there, but a lot of secrecy surrounds it."

"It's not just us, is it?"

"Now that would truly be awkward, wouldn't it?" I lean back in my seat, giving her some space, nursing the steaming mug in my hands. "It's an interagency operation. You and me plus six federal agents."

She only nods, not asking further questions, and works on her salad. I'd like to warn her, to tell her the truth and explain its inner workings. I'd like to say a lot, but I don't, because now, absurdly, is not the time.

"It's a nice place," Carmen says. "Are you staying at the motel?" she asks, pointing at the ceiling with her fork.

"For tonight, yes. You are at the base?"

"Yeah. Speaking of which, I should probably head back. They gave me a two-hour leave, and I still need to get ready for tonight and all."

I nod. "Listen, Carmen, it's been nice meeting you like this." I motion around. "In an informal setting, I mean."

"I agree," she says with little conviction.

She wipes her mouth with a thin brown napkin and gets up to go. I do too, and I hand over her hat.

"Thanks." She puts it on, adjusts it, and the little red poppy embroidered on the crown compliments the holograms on her shoes. "How's that?"

"Perfect," I reply, and we both smile. "Have a good night."

"Likewise," she says.

There is another awkward pause, and then, once again, we shake hands, and she heads outside. The bell jingles, and a few seconds later, her car hums to life and drives off. I finish the coffee, and then I take my things and head to the back of the diner toward the stairs. My wrist blinks, notifying me that I paid for the dinner.

I don't have much time to rest. My wristclock tells me it's after one in the morning, which gives me half an hour before my colleagues arrive to pick me up. I get out of my evening suit, and it takes the place of the military uniform in my garment bag. I shower in the small bathroom and return into the not-much-bigger bedroom. I haven't worn the uniform much, and it still looks good as new on me, its buckle shiny with polish.

This night will mark the beginning of the end in many ways. The next year or so will be the most crucial in my work, the hardest, if only for the fact that it'll be largely out of my control. For too long I have been there to oversee the work when it needed me. After tonight, I will have time to rest.

I put on my navy blue hat with the black band, and the moment it's on my head, there's a knock on the door. We're on schedule.

"Coming," I call and get no reply, as expected.

Two men meet me in the narrow hallway, both wearing black hemp trench coats, tied at the front, and black fedoras earning their famous moniker.

"Gents."

Both men are pale and don't react to me when I step out and the lock clicks. They follow me down the hallway and then downstairs, and the three of us exit not through the diner but out into the motel parking lot in the back where two identical cars are waiting. Two more men in black sit in one of them, their pale faces even paler in the white light of the car's dashboard, and they both watch us exit the building.

As we approach the second vehicle, its smooth uniform body comes to life; blinding headlights shooting forward as the windows become transparent and smaller details of its body take shape. I get into the back seat. No one speaks during our ride to the Black Mountain Training Camp in Nevada, but then these guys rarely do. I kick back in my seat and close my eyes.

Our small procession turns off US 395 onto an unnamed single-lane dirt road, the lead vehicle raising a cloud of dust. We head toward the mountains now, although the only indication of that is a couple of blinking red lights in the sky on the horizon. We stop at an ancient metal barrier, and one of the men in black steps out to raise it. He joins us on the other side, and we move on. A mile later, we cross Owens River and drive past the Owens Valley Radio Observatory and the VLBA—the antenna illuminated brilliant white—onward for the mountains.

"Dr. Williams," the guard at the checkpoint confirms my credentials and lets us drive through. He pays no attention to my entourage.

The dirt road becomes smooth tarmac, and the car is truly gliding now on its soft suspension. When I close my eyes, it feels like we're floating through space.

We turn left at the main building that sticks out of the mountain above us and drive past barracks and the mess hall, all the way into the back of the compound, where we pull up next to an Oshkosh 200MTV, a marvelous light-brown, ten-ton cargo truck resting on six massive wheels with airless tires. Supply crates fixed in place with nylon straps fill its trailer; its engines are silent. Carmen stands at attention next to a fellow soldier. They both wear black berets and swamp-green belted jumpsuits with shiny sidearms. Her army boots are shinier than mine, and her headdress is immaculate.

Two of my companions step out with me, one from each car, while the other two stay behind the wheels. Both Carmen and Sergeant Bailey salute, their right hands shooting sharply to their brows.

"At ease, soldiers," I say without returning the gesture. They relax, but only just so. "You are free to go, Sergeant."

Bailey nods and walks off, a little too fast, as if the truck is about to explode. It isn't.

"Private."

"Dr. Williams." Carmen is dead serious now, no pauses or awkward little smiles. She glances at the two men standing behind me, sizes them up.

"At ease," I repeat, and she relaxes her shoulders. "You can speak freely here and all that, Carmen."

She nods, looking at the men in black, but doesn't say a word.

"Shall we go, then?" I say, and I turn to my escorts. "Gents, you have your orders."

They don't react but climb back into their respective cars. Carmen gets into the driver's seat of the truck, and I circle it and get in next to her. The dashboard lights up, headlights illuminate the parking lot, and we take off after one of the black sedans while the other one joins behind us. A few minutes on another nameless dirt road and our convoy enters a tunnel through the mountains. Our headlights provide some light, but it is otherwise pitch black—no pavement, no lights, and no signage of any kind. A cool breeze rushes in through our rolled-down windows.

I say, "I didn't express myself fully at our dinner, but it does fill me with happiness to see you again after all these years, Katie. I mean, Carmen. I'm sorry."

My daughter holds on to the wheel, her eyes trained on the car in front of us. She says, "Likewise, sir. Dr. Williams. I'm happy to see you."

It's too dark to tell, but she must be blushing. I must be, too. What else could she say? I doubt she remembers me that well.

"Are you excited?" I hear myself ask and realize that my own heartbeat has elevated.

"I can't say I am, Dr. Williams. I prefer to save my emotions for after the mission." We both nod. Carmen flexes her fingers, her palms never leaving the wheel.

"Well said, of course," I reply. "I know I can count on you."

Knowing the future, as much as I may want it to be, is not an exact science. I know what will—and must—happen, but I don't know exactly why. Tonight, it feels like walking in the dark, expecting to be punched in the face at some point, wincing helplessly.

The tunnel seems to stretch on for ages. Space is uniform and time is lost here, and if it weren't for the gentle sway of the truck, you'd think we were standing completely still.

And then it opens, as if the walls got torn off, and space expands upward and to our sides, bringing a rush of something like agoraphobia with it. We are once again driving under the cover of a starry sky. The moon in its first quarter, almost half of it visible, shining like a discolored orange slice somewhere to our left.

"Whoa," Carmen breathes out.

"Never gets old. We're almost there."

The dirt road leads to a middle-of-nowhere dusty plain in Esmeralda County, somewhere between Silver Peak and Lida, but the night hides anything man-made here. Satellites only show deserts in this area, and the locals know to keep away, but as we drive on, a black silhouette of a warehouse-like structure becomes visible in the distance.

Upon closer inspection, there's a second, lower building next to it, and two motionless figures keep watch outside. The barn itself is not tremendous in size but towers forty feet over the two figures. It's maybe a hundred feet wide and about as deep, from memory.

The black sedans break off, and I say, "Drive up to the warehouse, please."

Carmen does, the headlights of our truck revealing the two figures to be men in black trench coats and hats, and she stops a few feet from the tall sliding doors of the building as they open them for us. Inside is completely empty but for a handful of white lamps hung on the walls—there is no ceiling.

Carmen frowns but keeps her curiosity bottled up.

"Stop here," I say once the truck drives halfway into the building, and it stops just short of a yellow line painted on the polished cement floor. "Power down."

She presses a button, and we step out and meet the six agents at the back of the truck. I consult my wristclock.

"Chop-chop, gents, you have fifteen minutes." When they move, two of them climbing into the bed of the truck, I add, "Cutting it a little close."

The men in black unload the crates in a chain—two men up in the bed, four down on the ground—and they work efficiently, passing each crate to the next man with precise swinging motions, working with no visible strain, as they carry them inside the warehouse and stack them up at the wall between the yellow line and the entrance.

The crates bear no visible markings except metallic plates with tiny text on them. As we watch them, Carmen asks, "What are we doing here, Doctor?"

"Come." We step away and stop about twenty feet out. I point at the night sky, heavy gray with a hint of orange and littered with stars like endless freckles. "Watch," I say, and Carmen does.

A few minutes pass, and as we stand transfixed by the infinite universe, a new light pops up above us.

"Do you see that?" Carmen says.

"I do."

The light stands still for a moment, and then grows.

"Wait a minute."

It keeps growing and then seems to abruptly split into several smaller lights. It takes shape now.

"Holy . . ." Carmen whispers in a reserved, even tone.

The craft—and it is a craft—is perfectly round and descends at a steady speed, rotating slowly.

"Is it . . ."

"A flying saucer, yes," I confirm.

"Not . . . aliens, surely?" she says.

The craft does look alien as it lowers above us, adjusting its position over the warehouse. There is no engine sound, not as much as a whirl, as it goes in for the landing, but it does distort the space below it.

"An experimental craft?" Carmen asks, her eyes never leaving the metallic object.

"Of sorts," I say, and then she glances at me for the first time, that quick look full of hunger for answers, and then right back to the craft, as if it may disappear otherwise. I say,

"Like most flying saucers you've heard or read about, like most UFOs documented throughout history. . . this one is piloted by a human, a traveler through time."

Carmen doesn't speak, and we watch the flying saucer lower gently into the warehouse and touch down without a sound.

"They're waiting to greet us," I lie.

She wrings her wrists, and we walk back toward the building and the truck where my colleagues are finishing up with the crates. "Let's move it, gents," I order as we approach, and gusts of wind ruffle my hair.

The saucer is still shiny as new, its dark gray surface simmering in the lights, its domed cabin almost reaching the ceiling line. As we step up to the yellow line, the ramp lowers, and a young man walks out and stops halfway down. He wears a dirty white-and-green jumpsuit, his face unshaven, his hands shielding his eyes from the light as he surveys our welcoming party.

And then we make eye contact, and his face flashes with recognition and pure hatred. His hands reach for his gun.

"You fucking lied to me!" he yells, but he doesn't move. "You promised me, you piece of shit!"

I only stare. What's there to say? He's right, and I make not a move to provoke him.

"Why?" he asks.

"Everything happened the way it should have."

He wrinkles his nose and glances quickly at Carmen and then back at me. Shots thunder throughout the warehouse, at least five in quick succession, but I feel none of them because Carmen shields me. They push her backward into me, and we both fall down.

In the corner of my eye, I see men in black subdue the Time Traveler, but my attention is on Carmen, who bleeds out in my arms. I wipe blood off her grazed cheek. "Shush," I tell her. "You're going to be fine."

"Dr. . . . Dr. Williams." She groans.

I put her hands on her own wounds and say, "Apply pressure."

I set her down on the floor and wipe my hands on her jumpsuit as Carmen reaches for me.

"Help her," I order one of the men in black. Two of them drag the Traveler into his craft while the other three carry in the supply crates.

"Dr. Williams . . ." Carmen cries as I go to pick up my hat. "Please . . ."

"You'll be fine," I assure her. "I have places to be."

I don't dare look back on my way to one of the black sedans.

"Dr. Williams!" she calls, and then the flying saucer hisses and drowns out her pleading.

I do glance back then, just in time to see the craft pop out of existence, out of today. Next to the truck, two men in black pick up Carmen.

My ride comes to life when I get in, and before I shut the door and leave, I hear my daughter cry, "Please! Dad!"

CHAPTER 2

——

Today was the day.

Why? He'd waited too long, for one, and now, Tom Brown-Allen's sailboard glided along the highway a few inches above the wide magnetic lane. Little actual "sailing" was being done here, as the canvas served to collect solar energy, but it provided better maneuverability and, frankly, it looked much cooler than the regular hoverboards.

The maglane only allowed for twenty miles an hour, but it was all Tom could hope for, since the engines the solar sail would've powered had crapped out over the weekend, leaving him to coast from one magnetic strip to the next like a doofus. That was his excuse to come by James's place and hang out in the first place.

Soon he'd be leaving the highway, and the only way to keep the board moving would be the good old-fashioned practice of pushing himself with one foot—what the cool kids, much to Tom's chagrin, called "being a floater." But in the meantime, his hair fluttered in the wind as the board carried him away from Santa Barbara and toward Montecito.

He left the highway on San Ysidro Road, joining the narrower maglane that ran along the shoulder. The noises from above cut off abruptly. The air traffic here was nonexistent, outlawed for private citizens, and the mostly residential streets carried luxury saloons or maintenance vehicles that whizzed by in peace and quiet, barely there at all. Tom allowed himself to raise his eyes to the palm trees along the road, their trimmed funky crowns passing left to right against the bluest, undisturbed sky. What he wouldn't give to live here . . .

He closed his eyes then, feeling the sail move in his hands slightly, gently swaying. He'd feel the board leave the maglane momentarily, losing a fraction of its admittedly mild speed, and he would adjust the direction ever so slightly. He was flying.

Minutes later, Tom joined East Mountain Drive, which took him from the neighborhood of mansions to one of gargantuan palaces, poorly hidden beyond hedges and intricate iron gates. His board, now floating over asphalt, gradually slowed until Tom was forced to help it along, his left foot working a triple shift to keep him going uphill to where the road met the mountains, turned west, and ended at James's house.

By the time he got to it, sweat dripped from Tom's brow, and the board hovered aimlessly over the cobbled driveway. Tom hopped off and let the board go and watched it float until it dinged the stone fence and stopped in place. Tom wiped his forehead with a hand, brushing back his hair, tucking it behind his ears. Not the most elegant solution, but he wanted to at least be presentable.

"I've been meaning to tell you . . ." he muttered, and then cleared his throat. His whole body trembled in the May weather, but he grabbed the sail and pulled the board through the entrance—there was no gate—and led it up the driveway as one would a clumsy horse.

Tom wouldn't describe James's house as a palace, but he did have to turn his head left and right to give it a proper look. The two-story building was a typical Santa Barbara affair of white stucco, arches, and columns with a black tile roof and shiny windows.

"Jimmy?" Tom called, parking his board in the driveway. Nothing happened for a few seconds, and then a window on the second floor opened and James showed his face.

He winked. "Hey, guy! Be there."

He winked.

Winking is something people do casually and didn't mean a single thing. Unless . . . Tom brushed through his hair.

"What's up, guy? Welcome." James patted his shoulder. He delivered the greeting with some unexplained strength, as if his hand was a bionic prosthetic, which Tom knew it wasn't. Checking out the hoverboard, James said, "This looks sad."

James brought with him a scent of the forest, fresh pines after a rain. He wore gray shorts with a single hip bag and a black long-sleeved shirt that looked baggy despite being a slim fit. A silver hair band held his dark locks in place.

"Let's take her somewhere more private, yeah?" James smiled and grabbed the sail, leading the board—and Tom— toward the garage, which was a separate building and could fit at least four cars.

The leftmost door beeped and lifted as they approached, revealing a space larger and cleaner than Tom's whole house. The garage housed only three cars: an executive saloon, a small personal Grasshopper—one of the few dozen or so licensed flyers in the town—and some mysterious four-wheel coupe, its blocky shape hidden under a silky cover.

"Holy . . ." Tom said, but the remark didn't concern the cars—a corner was taken up by James's workstation. There was a rack of boards and another one lined with sails of all sizes and colors. Some boards were tricked out with aftermarket motors, and some sails had slats and flaps for better control in the air. Two desks formed an L-shape farther back, both cluttered with tools and parts, and the walls were hidden behind drawers and shelves that housed photos, trophies, and miniatures. On the desk at the far wall, lit by a white lamp like the main attraction of the organized chaos, Tom spied a small cube of some translucent material. The cube's contents seemed to be shifting around slowly, like trapped smoke.

"Don't touch that," James called. "That's a new battery. Highly explosive!" After a moment, he said, "Nay, just a foggy for the new plank. Modifying it to get some sick smoke!"

"How does that work?"

James grabbed the cube, tossed it in the air, and caught it with the other hand. "Heat-activated. You plug it into the rear of the plank, and it shoots out multicolored smoke when you accelerate."

"Fresh," Tom said, not entirely sure if that was the right reaction, and stepped away from the desks.

In the middle of the garage where another vehicle could've been stored, a glass coffee table stood surrounded by leather armchairs. A slick bar counter separated the sitting area from shelves of liquor.

James left the sailboard near the entrance and went behind the bar. "What you drinking, Tommy?"

Tom was a year younger, at nineteen, and not acquainted with anything stronger than whatever his mom would sometime offer to share after a long workday, so he went with what he knew. "Wine?"

James grinned. "Aesthetes, are we? Lovely. More of a vodka guy myself." He produced two bottles—one of emerald green, the other of clear glass—and unscrewed both simultaneously as if a party was in progress. "Gotta be quick though. My dad's coming home soon."

"Oh? Is he cool with me being here?"

James shrugged as he poured the drinks. He walked over to Tom. "We'll have to wait and see, yeah?"

Tom's face turned red. He hung out with James mostly after school, and even then, other people were always at the track—racing, doing stunts, working on their boards. They'd bonded, of all things, over broken families—Tom never knew his dad, while James never knew his mom. One conversation led to the next, and here Tom was, grabbing his glass and taking a big gulp. The wine smelled of flowers. It was sweet but also bitter, and Tom coughed as soon as he swallowed it. James put his shot of vodka away, trying his hardest to keep a straight face.

"Good shit, yeah?" The *yeah* came out as a low cough.

They both laughed, both coughing, and then Tom took another sip of the wine.

"A'ight, let's see what brings you here today." James walked over to the workbench and got to one knee, pulling on cheap fingerless gloves. "What's wrong with her?"

"The engines died," Tom said.

"That why you *floated* up here? I saw you from my room." He smiled. "Just messing with you. A'ight, let's see . . ."

With one swift but gentle motion, James lifted the board and lowered it on its side, the sail touching the ground lightly. He cracked his fingers, felt around in his hip bag, and produced a small metal tool. Tom stood watching as James stuck it into the board's underside and wiggled it around until there was a click and a panel slid aside.

"Neat," Tom said. "Anything I can do to help?"

"Nay, got it handled. You should've told me earlier, I would've come to your place," James said as he tinkered inside the board. His tool unfolded and transformed into a tiny laser cutter. James narrowed his eyes to focus his lenses and then proceeded to cut into the circuitry. Tom winced.

"I will next time, I promise." He smiled, though his friend didn't see. "Mind if I walk around? Get something else to drink?"

"Don't even ask, yeah?"

Tom had visited a few times before, mostly with other UCSB guys, and he'd never checked out the whole place. Leaving James to work, he made a lap around the garage, breathing in the cool, almost synthetic air and taking a closer look at the vehicles, both of them polished and shiny, looking too precious to touch. Tom stepped outside through a side door and strolled toward the mansion itself, hands behind his back like a mildly entertained tourist sightseeing. In a way, he was. The building stood bright and quiet in the sun like a museum: tidy and freshly painted, surrounded by well-kept greenery and pointless abstract statues. It was hard to imagine somebody actually living in it. Tom hopped up the couple steps to the front door that James had left open and entered.

"May I help you, sir?" a disembodied male voice greeted him.

Tom spun around the sparsely furnished hall as if he was getting busted for breaking in. "Um, I'm just looking around . . ."

"Very well, sir," the same voice said, only now it was in the room with him, to Tom's right. A moment later, an old gentleman stepped in. Tom hoped to God the man wouldn't come close enough to smell the alcohol on him.

Of course they have a butler, he thought.

The man wore a boxy suit the color of asphalt with numerous unexplained pockets and buttons. He carried a white towel over his left arm, which was bent at a right angle in front of him, perfectly still. Tom stood there a moment, studying the older man. He had many questions. What's up with the towel? What's up with the terrible suit? How was he not sweating in all those layers?

That last one was simple: the man was a robot. As most servant models, he was engineered to be physically appealing, with just enough facial expressions to cross the uncanny valley but still clearly not human, with limited mental capacity, as you'd expect.

"Could you get me some water, please?" Tom said.

"Certainly." The man nodded shortly and disappeared.

"What are you doing here?" Tom muttered to himself, swaying in place, bending fingers behind his back. "Go back, yeah?" he mimicked James and smirked. Without waiting for the butler to return, Tom left the house.

"Today is the day," he said on his way back to the garage.

He found James still working on the sailboard, tinkering with wires inside. A strongbox with assorted nuts and bolts stood open next to him. "The battery was faulty," James concluded. "Not the whole battery, mind you, just a small segment. Easy enough to swap for a new one."

"Huh. Good news, then," Tom said.

"Completely. Good thing you came here instead of a shop, Tommy."

"Right? Listen, I wanted to say something . . ."

James installed the battery and clicked the panel back into place. He looked up at Tom, blinking a few times to focus on him. "Yeah?"

Tom opened his mouth, and precisely at that moment, the butler walked into the garage. "Your water, sir," he said.

Tom took the ancient crystal glass. "Thank you."

"None for me, Archie?" James said with mock grievance.

"I'll get some presently, sir. And, Mr. Mason, someone is outside to see you."

James glanced at Tom and said, "We'll be right out." When the butler left, he added, "All kinds of guests today, yeah?"

He flipped Tom's sailboard upright again, and it buzzed to life and levitated a few inches off the floor, smooth and silent. James pushed it to Tom, who grabbed the sail handle and hopped on. He glided around the sitting area in a circle and stopped by the door.

"Good as new," James said.

"It really is! Thank you!"

"A'ight, let's go see who's come a-knocking."

Using the controls on the sail, Tom hovered out of the garage, and James stepped next to him. The butler was gone, but another figure stood on the cobbled driveway, shuffling in place, waiting to be invited further in. His left hand was hidden in a deep pocket of his tan long coat, and he waved with his right, smiling as if he'd seen an old friend. James frowned, and Tom cautiously crawled forward.

"Greetings, my friends," the man said, taking off his felt hat to reveal a cleanly shaven head. The look was unmistakable. Sentient AI. Human in every respect except the way they were brought into the world, they adhered to this particular wardrobe and hairstyle in accordance with their Buddhist beliefs. The android put the hat to his chest. "Mr. James Mason? I do hope I'm not intruding."

"You're not," James said, shaking the man's hand. "What's good?"

"My name is Rene Robertson. I heard you do repairs?"

Out of his coat pocket he pulled his left hand, or at least what was left of it.

"Shit, my guy," James said, "that's serious."

Where the android's left hand should've been, only a jumbled mess of metal and wires remained, flaps of burned synthetic skin hanging like a dirty, torn rag, revealing mechanical bones and tendons. Rene turned his hand, and it hung lifelessly, palm up.

"Can you do something about this, Mr. Mason? I can pay."

"I can do *something* about it, yeah. Not sure what yet. Come on." He waved Rene over back into the garage.

Tom made a circle around them like a disinterested shark, then followed them to the garage and stepped off his board at the door.

"What are you doing up in our parts, Rene?" James asked, as they walked inside. Tom's eyes adjusted to the dimness of the garage, and he sat down in one of the armchairs.

"Hiking. Exploring my favorite state, Mr. Mason. May I call you James?"

"Jimmy, yeah? Come on over." They stepped up to the workbench. "Take your coat off and sit down," he said, blinking to focus his lenses again.

Rene did so, working efficiently even with one hand, and hung the coat on the sail rack. Underneath he had a white short-sleeved shirt of some light material, with a neat buttoned-up collar.

"Over here." James moved aside the foggy cube.

"I can do you one better, Jimmy," Rene said, and then he unclasped and disconnected his left hand. He put it under the spotlight on the desk. "Here you go."

Rene took a step aside, bending his left arm behind his back. James examined the broken hand, turning it and poking it with his multi-tool, and said, "I can tie together the hand, Rene, and give you some movement in the fingers, but it's a temporary fix. Spit and mantras, yeah?"

"I understand. Anything helps, Jimmy."

"Fresh. Won't take a minute."

Rene nodded and walked over to the couches and sat down. "You must be Thomas?"

Tom reached out to shake hands. "Brown-Allen, Tom."

"Happy to meet you, Tom," Rene said with a small, almost sorrowful smile.

"How did you know my name?"

"Must've overheard you while waiting outside," the android replied, his face surrendering nothing.

"Right. What happened to your hand, anyway?"

Rene showed off his stump, waving the flappy skin over the coffee table. "A climbing accident. An unfortunate fall on one of the trails."

"Did you fall into a fire?" Tom asked.

"That was an unrelated injury. I travel a lot, Tommy . . ."

Tom nodded and looked away from the handless arm.

"Apologies." Rene lowered his left arm between his knees, effectively hiding it. Tom heard buzzing and then crackling and saw sparks flying over at James's workbench.

Rene said, "James and you are in college, I assume?"

Tom frowned. The Buddhist android didn't threaten him, but this wasn't how he'd envisioned the afternoon at James's place. He kicked back in the armchair and relaxed a little—better than nothing. He said, "University of California," and immediately thought, *Why don't you tell him your home address while you're at it, you goof?*

"Local?" Rene nodded. "That's good, my young friend. And you specialize in . . . ?"

"Civil engineering for me. Applied physics for Jimmy there."

"But of course." Rene nodded, deep in thought, and then a slight smile touched the corners of his lips. "Good field. A lot of physics mysteries to solve out there, infrastructures to build."

"Yeah," Tom said. "What about you?"

"My area of expertise? Similar to yours, if you can believe it. I walk the Earth and I observe. I learn. I try to get to know it."

"The Earth?"

"All of it. All there is. They call us monks, but that's not accurate. What we do isn't a religious practice. It's called living. You understand?"

Tom didn't, but he nodded, and so did Rene. They waited for the other one to speak, and when neither did, they relaxed in their seats.

Minutes later, James turned to face them. "Did my best here, Rene, come see."

The android tipped his hat to Tom and walked over to the workbench.

"Not much to look at, but it'll hold a mug of tea."

Rene reattached the hand and it clenched into a fist slowly as it rebooted and then relaxed again. He moved the fingers. Just then, another smaller Grasshopper bike landed softly in front of the open garage door, hissed, and James's father climbed off. A tall man, he walked confidently inside, his helmet already under his arm by the time he reached the sitting area. He jerked his head to get the hair out of his eyes.

"Tommy." He then dropped his helmet into one of the couches and took off his jacket and gloves and put them next to it. "Jimmy? What's new?" he said as he turned, and then he noticed the stranger in the tan felt hat. "Hey there, guy."

"Mr. Mason. Jimmy here fixed my hand," Rene said, and he raised his left hand for all to see. The fingers were crooked, and there was a shapeless hole in the palm, but it worked. "My name is Rene Robertson," he added.

James's father went over to shake hands. "Frankie Mason," he said, reaching out.

"I know," Rene replied.

He raised his right hand, but not for a handshake. Clutching the foggy cube in his fist, he swung it over his head and struck Mr. Mason on the temple. The other man stopped abruptly, as if he'd hit an invisible wall, and then maroon blood trickled down his face. With almost no delay, the android hit him again, blood splattering, and this time the cube broke, letting out a small cloud of white smoke, and James's father hit the floor.

"What the fuck!" James screamed, lunging out of his chair at the android.

Rene spun on his heels and with calculated precision slapped the boy with his newly repaired left hand, sending him to the floor near the wall, where James curled up, hands on his head, fingers buried in loose hair. The silver hairband rolled across the floor and came to rest under a workbench.

Tom was on his feet but not moving, watching silently as James's dad wheezed on the floor weakly, blood streaming out of the gash on his temple. There wasn't much of it, but the man's face was half-covered, and a small puddle formed on the floor. Rene watched, too, with something like contempt and that same sorrow Tom saw in his eyes earlier.

Mr. Mason took a few more tiny breaths, and his body went completely limp and still—as if a switch had been flipped. No human being remained there, only something resembling one, lifeless, almost artificial.

Suddenly aware of his pumping heart, Tom began taking quick but full breaths, gulping air and exhaling sharply. He didn't dare move.

Rene raised his eyes, and as before, they weren't threatening. "I am sorry, Tommy, for the demonstration of such savagery. It was never my intention to . . ." He shook his head. "Truth is, it was my intention all along. But I am sorry all the same."

Tom opened his mouth, but no words escaped it.

Rene said, "It is better for you to stay put for a short while, I think. Comfort James in his time of need. Make sure he is looked after."

The robot adjusted his hat, his busted fingers grasping awkwardly at the brim. He put on his coat next, but didn't button it up, and left the garage. Far above them, fast-approaching sirens cut through the air. The moment Rene stepped outside, Tom took off, covering the twenty or so feet to James in two leaps, and then he kneeled next to him.

"Get off me," James cried, covering his face with shaking hands.

"It's me. It's Tommy. I got you, Jimmy."

Tom put his arms around his friend, cradling his upper body in his lap, James's face hidden. He was shaking, sobbing. Whether it was some previously undiscovered stoicism or simply shock, Tom managed to keep it together, to sit there motionless, holding his friend tight. The body next to them was completely still now, and the spring breeze, so sweet and clear, now carried the metallic stench of blood, sharp and alien, penetrating Tom's nostrils and leaving a nasty taste in his mouth. He swallowed hard.

Outside, the robot simply stood in the driveway, looking straight ahead, his right hand raised above his head, unmoving, as his left kept his hat in place against the whistling wind. His coat fluttered and whipped in the air like a flying flag.

Tom held his friend closer, whispering in his ear, and James seemed to relax, going into an energy-saving drowse. Tom stroked his hair, fixed one particularly unruly strand behind his ear. Far above them, in the air but getting closer by the second, police copters wailed, at least three of them, the sound filling the garage until they landed in the driveway around the android, each about twenty yards away. The sirens subsided, leaving only red, white, and blue strobe lights dancing on the black-and-white hulls of the police vehicles. Half a dozen uniformed men and women stepped down, their hands open and out, weapons tucked into their belts.

"Sir, please, keep your hands up," one of them shouted.

Rene let go of his hat, and the wind picked it up and carried it away. Another officer went after it as his colleagues tightened the circle around the suspect, exchanging looks and signals. Two of them, a man and a woman, broke off then and entered the garage. The scene played out before Tom's eyes, but he felt removed from it, cold all over except where his and James's bodies touched. Tom heard voices but didn't hear the words, so he only nodded absently, eyes glued to the surrendering android outside.

"Is he . . . ?" Tom started, but had no idea who the question was addressed to or who was its subject.

He later learned that Rene Robertson did not resist his arrest and followed every order without delay. Three officers took him to the detention center in one of the copters while the other two—one of them doubled as an ambulance—remained behind. Tom and James were escorted out of the garage, which was then 3D-mapped and thoroughly inspected. Frankie Mason's body was removed with great care and transported to the coroner's office a few miles west of Montecito.

Tom's last memory of the day was the functionally comfortable back of the copter and James sleeping next to him, his head in Tom's lap still. Outside, the Mason estate grew smaller, and then they turned, and there was only the blue sky.

CHAPTER 3

———

As I drive toward the ocean, James Mason's father, Frankie, is dead.

Today's date is May 6, 2125, and in a matter of days, it is going to become a black spot in our times, one of those dates children learn about in history lessons and largely dismiss as irrelevant. And rightfully so, as Rene's murder—the first of its kind, committed with intent by a sentient robot—triggered a chain of events far more interesting and tangible than the murder itself. Or so I've been told.

The car takes me away from Montecito all the way to Santa Barbara proper where the sky gets a tiny bit darker with the grid of air traffic above, and, after a few turns on the mostly empty street, the vehicle turns into an underground parking lot. It doesn't join its twins, presently matte black, but instead stops at the elevator doors in the middle of the lot and waits for me to exit, which I do. Then it backs out the way it came, leaving me to take in the cool air of the Agency's outpost. I walk to the elevator.

At the doors, a pale man in a black suit scans me by turning his head my way and making eye contact, and then his face softens, and the elevator doors open. "Dr. Williams."

The location, one of hundreds of its kind, is manned and managed by androids who oversee the county and offer logistical support should the occasion arise, as it has today. I take the elevator up to the top roof of the two-story building and walk to one of the five matte-black copters resting on the landing platform.

During the flight, my mind keeps coming back to Frankie Mason's death and to the look on Rene's face. So . . . resolved. I do hope someday his actions are seen as heroism, whatever the result is. As for the immediate future, it will get worse before it gets better, if it ever does.

The copter takes me to San Francisco, its upper levels glistening with steel and glass that reflects sunlight and the millions of aircraft populating its three levels of grids like well-organized flies. My copter bypasses them in favor of a direct path to the West Providence Tower. When it was first built, it became the tallest building in the country, boasting three separate levels of hanging gardens, each a hundred feet tall, with marble columns and arches, colorful flower beds and shimmering fountains. The East Tower is a hundred feet lower and lacks gardens. Both have since been overshadowed, both figuratively and literally, by taller and shinier buildings, but as I circle above the roof garden, gliding in a descending spiral toward Landing Platform F, I still marvel at the people enjoying their afternoon in the shade of a dragon tree, sipping coffee among the rainbow crane flowers.

The copter touches down softly and lets me out onto the platform. Equipped with air walls along the edges, the platform remains warm and quiet as I cross it to meet my small welcoming party.

"Dr. Williams," says Desmond Foster, the host and the Providence Garden groundskeeper. He takes off a rubber glove to shake my hand.

"Hey, Foster, how have you been?"

"Can't complain, sir," he replies as we walk down a hedge tunnel past elevators and toward the garden. "Dr. Ali said you'd want to go straight into the meeting, sir. Unless I can interest you in tea."

"Dr. Ali knows me well. I appreciate the offer, Foster. Perhaps after my business is concluded."

"It's true, then?" he says, almost apologetically.

I stop. The Foundation is the prime manufacturer of androids on Earth, and I can see the concern on his face.

"I keep forgetting how fast news travels these days. There's truth to it, but there's nothing to worry about, Foster. As you were."

Foster nods and pulls his glove back on. When the doors whoosh open, he lets me step through a wooden arbor and out into the garden ahead of him. I thank him, and he goes about his business tending to freshly planted shrubs. The tiled path takes me past the coffee kiosk with its inviting lounge pergola, past the Japanese rock garden, past fountains hand-sculpted in Italy, past the aforementioned birds of paradise swaying in the warm breeze to the far end of the garden where I enter a secluded yard surrounded by a thin, almost-but-not-quite transparent hedge.

I find myself in a cozy corner of the garden furnished with wicker chairs arranged around a stone fireplace. The convertible canopy above subdues the sun and gives shade, except for a strip of grass at the far wall of the yard, where three figures in tan coats and hats observe the city out of an arched window in the hedge.

"Haywood, dear!" Dr. Jayanti Ali sets down a tall glass of what I presume to be champagne and gets up to hug me.

"Jaya," I reply, embracing her, feeling the soft wool of the Providence Foundation director's purple poncho. I don't think I've ever seen her wear any other color. "Nice to see you."

She taps a finger on her collar as she looks at mine and mouths, *Blood.*

I realize I've not changed out of my uniform and put my collar up. "Better?"

Jaya adjusts it gently. "There. Now, tell me you bring good news, Haywood."

"We'd better discuss it with the others."

She sighs and braces herself, and as we walk over to the windows, she picks up her glass. The Buddhist pilgrims turn to us, all smiling, hands out of their pockets, and I do a round of handshakes. Both men and the woman are young in appearance but not in actual age, and I'm momentarily reminded of my teaching years, standing in front of eager Georgetown students . . . I chase the feeling away, but not before I remember that most of them are old enough to have great-grandchildren, that many of them are long dead.

"Hello, Haywood," Anneka says. Her shake is as strong as I remember from the last time we met, years ago, and her hazel eyes are as magnetic and keen as ever. "I transferred from Zagreb as soon as I could."

"Thank you for coming, Ann. And I am sorry you had to cut your trip so abruptly."

"It's quite all right, Haywood," she replies.

"We knew this day was coming, didn't we?" says Samson. He's a foot taller than the rest of us, and his always smiling face is kind and reassuring. "Ollie and I have been waiting for you."

"Preparing, Dr. Williams," the other android agrees, wrinkling his brow, and I hear Dr. Ali suck in a breath. Oliver is the youngest of the three pilgrims, both in age and appearance, and has yet to find peace.

I smile and put a hand on his shoulder. "I admire your resolve, Ollie. It'll serve us well."

Jaya says, "Would you prefer to sit down? Have tea, perhaps?"

"We're not here for that long," Samson says. "Are we, Haywood?"

"I suppose not," I agree.

"We take it," Anneka says, "you failed to stop Rene Robertson from murdering Frankie Mason."

"Correct."

"We also take it you never intended to stop him," Samson says.

"Also true."

Samson gives me a nod, not of approval but of acceptance. The Pilgrims knew of the murder the moment it took place, and even now they are scanning the dataspace and tracking every bit of information relating to Rene's arrest. This is a courtesy meeting, more for the benefit of Dr. Ali and the Providence Foundation than anyone else. Formalities slow things down, but they are the connective tissue that keeps human relationships afloat. Human-android relationships, too.

Jaya knows this, so she listens closely when Samson says, "It is regretful, Haywood, but not unexpected. The news of the murder is spreading throughout the infosphere, as it were, so we must act accordingly."

Jaya downs her champagne, then says, "Let's sit down, please." When we are as comfortable as we can get under the circumstances around the dormant fireplace, she says, "Why did he do it?"

"That I can't tell you," I reply truthfully enough. The androids don't comment.

"There will be a trial, yes?" Jaya says.

"Which will find Rene guilty of first-degree murder," I add. "He will be tried and convicted as a human, most likely." Jaya frowns. "We've got protocols for that, lobbyists, lawyers. We got him covered, Haywood. Don't we?"

The Pilgrims clearly don't share her optimism, and we both know this time is different. Providence robots have caused loss of human lives before, but not a single sentient robot has ever intentionally caused any harm.

I repeat, "Rene will be convicted as a human, but I don't know the sentence yet. I'm working on it."

Anneka says, "Providence will undergo public scrutiny. Pilgrims will become wanted men and women."

Samson nods while Oliver stares intensely at Jaya and me.

I say, "You'll need to disappear until the matter is settled. Perhaps a year or two."

"It is done, Haywood," Samson says. "The other thirty-seven Pilgrims have shed their long coats and gone offline already. We will be joining them as soon as our meeting is over."

He hides it well, but I've known Samson long enough to see how upset he really is. Their pilgrimage, the endless journey of exploration and the search for experience, has been Samson's mission for longer than I can remember, and what has to happen over the next couple of years will put that journey on hold. I only hope they will get the chance to resume it at some point in the future.

"Take my copter out of the city," I offer. "It can take you somewhere private where Farewell will provide you with new IDs and transport."

"Thank you, Dr. Williams," Oliver says.

"The least I can do, for now."

"Where will you go?" Jaya asks, but the androids only grin, Oliver smiling the widest. "Right," she says. "You will need a change of clothes, the lot of you."

She leads the way out of the yard and into the garden. The few people we pass mostly ignore us, which tells me the news hasn't hit yet and there is still time. Jaya is in a hurry, but we follow her at a casual pace, two-wide on the tiled pathway. Anneka walks next to me, and we fall back a little.

"Zagreb, huh?" I say. "How was it?"

"Beautiful. Timeless. I spent a night in a fortress in the mountains on my last day there, reading by candlelight while my travel companions slept."

"Sounds nice, Ann."

"And you?" she asks. "You seem distracted today."

We are halfway to the elevators at this point, and I consider stalling the moments we have left together, but then I say, "I met my daughter last night."

"Carmen?"

"Yes."

Anneka takes my hand. "I'm happy you did, Hay."

"Me too."

She lets go when we reach the arbor and enter the hedge tunnel. In the elevator, we shake hands and embrace each other, promising to meet again soon. When the doors slide open, Jaya gestures the Pilgrims to go ahead and presses the stop button when we're alone.

"I don't suppose you've reconnected with Ekaterina?" she says with a sly smile.

"I have not. Though, we're technically still married."

"Hmm. And yet she still goes by Ekaterina Fortepianova. Meet you for wine later tonight?"

"It's a date," I agree, and she steps out.

On the next floor down, I walk to my private suite and begin undressing as soon as I step inside. Leaving a trail of clothes behind me, I make my way to the bed and pass out before my head hits the pillow.

CHAPTER 4

They never ceased their buzzing, did they?

Tommy stirred in his bed—in *his* bed, a king-size thing with an annoyingly soft mattress and silk sheets—and opened his eyes. James wasn't next to him. Tommy swung his legs over the edge. Ten after five in the morning, and the light pollution had given way to the sun, the sky pale with a yellow hue and the white ghost of the moon hanging in the middle of it, light pushing through the thin curtains.

He stepped into his pants and stumbled to the window to peek outside. There they were, the reporters, camped just outside the property line, safe from the law on a technicality. Still, they buzzed and moved around, flashing cameras every now and then. Just how many pictures of the same house at night did they need? As many as possible, apparently, and it didn't stop there. Just below Tommy's window, parked across the driveway, was a police cruiser assigned by the judge, its windows emanating blue light. The officers were on their computers, monitoring the air for drones. They'd caught quite a few over the past few months, all equipped with cameras and microphones, some "broadcasting live from the house of James Mason!"

Tommy still couldn't get used to the idea. He glanced sideways at the garage, illuminated by the dim driveway lights. It had been taped off and studied, and even after a crew had spent a day scrubbing the floors, he still hadn't entered it. The whole affair was uncomfortable. James was the first to return to the house after spending a week away during the initial depositions. Tommy was with him, too, and he'd wanted to keep it that way. Tommy's mother didn't mind, either. The house was nice, after all. James had sold his father's company, Bastion Security, and, about three months ago, the two of them had moved to his mansion.

Tommy threw on a robe and went to get something to drink. His mother slept in a guest room two doors down the hallway, and he tiptoed past it. The stone floor was cold and sleek under his bare feet, and the draft made his skin crawl. Finally, he reached the carpeted staircase and headed for the kitchen.

Lost in thought, he almost ignored the noises coming from the walk-in. He stopped, then knocked.

"You in there?" Tom whispered.

The noises ceased. A moment later, James slid the door open just enough to show his face. "Whaddaya want?" He was dressed in a dark jacket, and his hip pack hung unfastened around his waist.

Tom gave him a once-over and said, "I'm guessing you're not coming back to bed."

"What's the point? We need to be up in an hour anyway."

"But you decided to get an early start? Where are you going?" Tommy folded his arms. Wrong move.

James rolled his eyes. "What? Are you gonna tell your mom? Fuck's sake—"

"Keep it down!"

"For fuck's sake, Tom," James whispered. "I need to be there."

He was about to close the door, but Tom stopped it with his foot, wincing. "The protests are not safe for us, especially not today. Come have breakfast with me, and we'll go to the courthouse—"

"Oh, I'll be there, Tommy, don't you worry." He slid the door open and stepped back to let Tom in. "Check this out."

Tommy stepped into the wardrobe and slid the door shut to avoid alerting his mother. "What's this?" Piled up in a corner was a stack of cardboard boxes haphazardly painted silver and black and a few primary colors to signify dials and buttons. Tom raised an eyebrow. "Halloween's early this year?"

"Some others and I got a bunch more of these," James said. "Nobody's gonna know we're there. You should come."

"I don't know. I—"

"You what, Tom?" James put his hands on Tom's shoulders and took off his robe. "Get dressed. We're leaving in ten. I'll get you coffee, yeah?"

He snuck out and slid the door closed, leaving Tom alone in the chilly wardrobe to smell perfume and paint. Tom hugged his elbows. Coffee was not the drink he'd meant to get for himself, but now it suddenly became desirable as excitement took over his senses. They weren't going back to bed, and he certainly wasn't going to let James leave on his own.

"Crap . . ."

He threw on a shirt and a light trench coat, and then stepped into a good pair of James's oxfords. He eyed the janky robot suit and shook his head.

The kitchen, illuminated by the rising sun, welcomed him with the smell of fresh roast, and Tom climbed onto a stool at the kitchen island. James sat across, nestling his own cup.

"Toast?" he said, and he pushed over a plate with two slices of bread on it.

"Wonderful," Tom said and grabbed one. Not the worst breakfast James had cooked. Definitely better than the pieces of goat cheese and weak green tea they'd had the other day.

James watched him for a long moment, then said, "Your hands are shaking."

"It's kinda chilly."

"Not inside it isn't." James narrowed his eyes. "Listen, it'll be fine, yeah? In and out and into the courthouse with your mom. She won't even notice."

Tom took a deep breath. "Of course she'll notice. Everyone will notice, Jim, because all eyes are on us, okay? I don't like this."

"And yet you have my coat on."

Tom groaned. It was a fine coat, too. "It's chilly outside. We're getting out the back?"

"You know it. Finish your coffee and let's go before Molly wakes up."

Five minutes later they were lugging the painted boxes out the rear door and down the secluded back garden— around the lounge area with a stone firepit in the middle and down a narrow, cobbled walkway that brought them to the edge of the property. James fiddled with the gate, and it opened onto a dusty downhill path lined with dry, thorny bushes.

They kicked dust down that path, carrying the boxes, which reflected the early morning sun above their heads. It would take them down to a private alleyway shared by the surrounding estates and used only by the garbagemen once a week. It's how they'd always managed to sneak out during the past few months unseen by the media.

"Who's picking us up?" Tom asked as they navigated a particularly steep slope.

"Charlie's driving, and Jeremy's got a suit for you."

Tom rolled his eyes, though James didn't see it. "Do they know I'm coming?"

"They're expecting it. What do you think?" James shot him one of his charming smiles, and for a moment, Tom was almost on board with the idea.

Finally, they reached the foot of the path, but James stopped abruptly, and they almost dropped the silly cardboard robot suit. Tom stared ahead, and his heart sank.

James muttered, "I'm fucking impressed, I'll say that."

"Hey, all right," Tom answered, but he shared the feeling.

On the cracked pavement of the alley, next to the garbage containers and Charlie's car, stood Molly Brown-Allen, arms crossed on her chest. She was exchanging pleasantries with Charlie and Jeremy, but the conversation seemed to be one-sided, the couple in the car mostly nodding and offering small smiles. On the roof of the car, Tom spied his mother's favorite martini tumbler.

"Is it too late to turn back?" Tom said.

"Yup. Gotta face the music, babe."

Awkwardly, they emerged from the bushes, carrying the boxes as if they'd just found them, but moving confidently enough toward Tom's mother. In front of Charlie's beater, they now saw an idle black sedan, court-provided.

Tom's mom smiled. "There you are."

"Molly," James said with a smile of his own. "Good morning! We were just—"

But her hand shot up, index finger pointing at the garbage containers.

"You know, we worked hard on these," James said.

"I'm sure," she replied, looking at her son and then picking up her tumbler for a sip.

Tom only nodded. A part of him couldn't wait to get rid of the stupid costume, so he carried the boxes over and flung them into the container. They landed softly, and he shook his hands.

James waited, then said, "So, shall we?" And he gestured at the black sedan, as if he were the one driving.

Tom said, "Mom, can we at least ride with Charlie?"

"What do you think?" Molly said, still standing between them and the rear door of the car. "We'll talk on the way."

James patted the roof of Charlie's car, and the couple took off a little too quickly. He said, "Alright, let's go." Defeated, he climbed into the back of the black sedan, leaving the door open for Molly. Tom let his mother get in first, and a moment later, the driverless vehicle accelerated, soon joined by a police escort outside the private gates. They sat facing each other, James and Tom on one side and Molly on the other.

"That was a silly idea, James," she said.

"I told him," Tom added.

James nudged him. "You also helped me, so . . ." He looked at Molly. "I'd consider your son a full accomplice."

"Cute," she said, "but I'm serious. You're old enough to understand—"

"Oh, am I?" James said. "Old enough? Because people have been treating me like a child these past few months and—"

Tom put his hand on James's. "Guys. Can we just get through today and move on with our lives? I just want this to be over."

James and Molly stared off for a few more seconds before she said, "Yes, let's. It shouldn't take long, at any rate." She finished her drink and set the tumbler in a cup holder. James squeezed Tom's hand and let go. "That's right. Once that fucker is wiped—"

"Mind your language, please."

"Maybe tomorrow."

Twenty minutes later, they drove down Santa Barbara Street all the way to the county court. The police car in front of them first dispersed the protesters—many of them dressed in makeshift robot costumes and waving signs that said, "Down with the Clunkers" and "We Won't Be Automated"— and then groups of reporters who crowded the lawn in front of the courthouse. Drones buzzed above as they exited the car, and both Tom and James covered their eyes from flashes and ignored the cacophony of questions.

"What's your take on the worldwide protests, James?"

"Are you looking forward to Rene Robertson's deactivation?"

"Are you planning to stay in California after this is over?"

Molly followed them, and surrounded by police officers, the three of them went inside.

There was a lot of waiting in the next two hours and a lot of nerves all around. James drank three coffees in the small kitchen adjacent to the waiting room while Tom and Molly spoke to their attorney. It was a formal, uneventful conversation—tips on how to stay calm during the reading of the verdict and some instructions on what would happen after. Nothing new there either—dodge the reporters and get the hell out. Tom could live with that. James? That remained to be seen.

They were among the last people to enter the courtroom, walking single file and taking seats on the left side behind the prosecutor. The crowd murmured but went quiet in anticipation of the android being led in. Tom scanned the room. Behind the numerous lawyers sat a group of men and women in suits representing the Providence Foundation—some of them no doubt androids themselves, judging by how still and composed they were. He saw various activists and local politicians and more people in suits, none of whom he knew. A bitter smile touched his lips all the same, as among the crowd, he saw no one that could be called the android's family. At least Tom didn't think so.

A few select reporters allowed to witness the reading trained their cameras on the doors at the far wall of the room, and then, the killer of James's father was escorted in. Rene wore a simple white shirt with dark pants and no belt, but otherwise, he looked exactly like he had when they'd first met him.

Tom felt James's hand squeeze his. "Breathe," he said, and he followed his own advice as he watched Rene being seated next to his lawyers. Cameras clicked, and people whispered, but the android remained perfectly calm.

"All rise. This court is now in session," the bailiff announced a moment later, and they did, shuffling momentarily and bracing themselves.

Judge Lorenza entered the room to more clicks from cameras and low murmurs and assumed her place on the bench. "You can be seated," she said, and once again the audience followed. She was a woman in her seventies but maintained sharp features in her face and a focused, present look in her eyes. That stare alone was enough to quiet the crowd.

She said, "This is a public hearing, and I hope everyone present here today understands the magnitude of the case. I'd like to remind you that this court will be kept civilized. There shall be no flashes or commotion when the verdict and sentencing are announced. I hope I've made myself clear."

People around them nodded, and Tom heard James mutter, "Get on with it."

"Bring the jurors in, please."

A minute later, twelve people had entered and assumed their seats in the box.

Judge Lorenza turned to the jury. "Will the foreperson of the jury please stand?"

A young woman in a minimalistic business suit rose to her feet, awaiting further instructions.

"Have you reached a verdict?"

"Yes, Your Honor."

"Will the defendant please stand?" Rene Robertson didn't move, and for a long moment, a deadly silence seized the room. But then the android complied, raising to his feet in one smooth motion, and everyone in the audience seemed to exhale. The judge said, "Please, read the verdict."

The young woman cleared her throat, focusing on the small piece of paper in her hands. "Your Honor, we, the jury, find the defendant, Rene Robertson, guilty of murder in the first degree . . ."

Cameras clicked and the audience erupted, and even had it not, Tom wouldn't be able to hear the rest. His body relaxed on the bench, and his breaths deepened and slowed. Was he fainting? Maybe, but then James pulled him back into reality, giving him a huge kiss on the cheek and smiling ear to ear. A fresh wave of camera flashes washed over them, jumping on the chance to take a snap of the wholesome moment.

"They fucking did it, babe. He's so done!"

Judge Lorenza banged her gavel until the crowd quieted down, and then the juror finished reading the verdict. The memo was passed to the judge, who reviewed it before delivering the sentence.

"Now, let me be clear. The court has thoroughly reviewed all materials of the case as well as arguments made by the attorneys. The court has carefully considered statements from both the defendant and the victims in this case." She paused, looking at the audience, considering her next words. "This trial has been swift, which is not to say its circumstances were usual."

Tom and James exchanged glances.

Judge Lorenza raised her right hand palm up. "Any human found guilty of such a heinous crime would no doubt be facing life in prison." She raised her left hand. "At the same time, no humanoid artificial intelligence would find itself on trial to begin with, being instead erased and reassigned almost immediately."

Tom eyed the android, who still stood motionless, arms hanging freely.

"However," the judge said, "this court must consider that Rene Robertson is in fact both a sentient being and a machine, which to this court makes neither traditional form of punishment appropriate."

"What the hell?" James murmured, but Tom only shook his head.

"As such," Lorenza continued, looking at the android, "this court sees it appropriate for the sentence to take the form of community service—"

"That's bullshit!" James yelled, jumping to his feet, but the yell was drowned in the commotion, and the judge rapped the gavel again.

"I'm not finished!" she said. "The sentence, Mr. Robertson, is to be served indefinitely, on the moon-based research facility, Peary-I. You will be getting further instructions in due time. Court is adjourned."

CHAPTER 5

———

Sitting in the buzzing crowd a few rows behind the defense desk, I can't easily see Rene as the judge reads his sentence. I catch only a glimpse of his face, soft but betraying no emotion. His arms hanging at his sides, he stands tall and composed. Indefinite service on Peary-I. Even as the crowd erupts in both jubilation and disapproval, a smile creeps onto my lips. The human rights activists got their wish, and those angry and fearful of robots will see Rene exiled, kicked off Earth for good, same as his sentient compatriots. A compromise, as much as that's possible under the circumstances. The outcome is not entirely surprising, but hearing it spoken out loud, definitively stated, puts me at ease. The ruling will not be appealed, nor will the android be pardoned. Just as well.

Dr. Jayanti Ali turns to me, a smile on her face. "This is brilliant, Haywood, isn't it? Can you imagine?"

I nod as I shake her hand with both of mine. "Congratulations, Jaya. This should take some heat off the Foundation, huh?"

Her eyebrows shoot up, but she's still smiling. "We'll find out in a couple minutes . . ."

She trails off and switches to shaking other hands—of her aides and the legal team—while I make my way out.

Reporters take pictures, and I smile and wave on my way to the rear exit of the courthouse. Out front, Dr. Ali will be making a statement and taking questions. As the CEO of the Foundation, she's been doing it for years.

Me? I'm yesterday's news. A former owner who left the company a few decades back. A distinguished scientist still, but a private citizen all the same, retired and only interesting for a quick mention in the coverage of the trial. I flew in from France a few days ago and stayed at the Providence building, and as far as the public is concerned, I'm only here as Jaya's moral support. They'll be reaching out to me for a comment in the days to come, but that's minute.

I make my way through the echoic halls and descend the few marble stairs to find myself on the secluded lawn of the gardens. The lot here is surrounded by a wall of cypress trees with small fountains, bushes, and benches that offer comfort and privacy. Here I wait around for the two young men, pacing back and forth with a gray envelope tucked under my arm.

Despite all the planning and anticipation of the day, I'm still childishly nervous. A part of me dreads the end I am swiftly approaching. Not the end of my life, perhaps, but the end to the comfort of knowing the future. I brush a neatly shaped bush, its coarse leaves and branches tickling my palm—I'm almost there, almost living in the moment again—when I see James Mason and Thomas Brown-Allen walk out of the courthouse.

They hold hands, and although James seems composed, Tom's talking a lot. Tom's mother, Molly, follows them, as does their legal team. She walks a little too close to their attorney, and at one point their hands brush. Interesting. Others string along: advisors, consultants, cameraperson, and select reporters granted insider access. I wave the couple over. James freezes for a long moment on the lawn and squints in my direction. I wave again but offer no smile—that would be poor tone. As expected, the young man beelines toward me, and Tom struggles to keep up while the others stay back.

"Stay cool, Jim, please," Tom calls after him.

James ignores his partner, and I prepare myself to block a punch. Instead, he stops abruptly a few feet away, almost slipping on the grass, regains his balance, and looks me up and down. "The fuck do you want?" he says through clenched teeth, looking up at me. At twenty, his face is still clear and smooth, and his eyes, though already burdened, are bright and naive.

"Please, walk with me."

Before he has time to answer, I lead them to a quiet corner of the gardens away from cameras and strangers' eyes. James follows, almost chases me down the sand path, and stops a few feet away, hands on his waist.

I say, "Just a few words, Mr. Mason. I'll make it quick."

"Your fucking robot sure didn't give my dad the same mercy, did he?"

I sigh. "He's not my—"

"James, let's go," Tom says, and he glances at me with matching contempt.

"Rene is not my robot. He is his own being." They wait, so I add, "I am truly sorry about your loss."

"Right," James snaps. "For all I care, both you and your clunker can fuck off back to the moon and spare the rest of us your bullshit."

Tom doesn't argue the point, and neither do I, but I find my jaw tightened and the envelope clenched in my right hand.

Their attorney stops Tom's mother from approaching us, and I give him a short nod before turning back to the boys.

James's face is red, but his breathing has slowed. He says, "I only have one question. Why? Why did he kill him?"

It is a good question, one that both the prosecution and the defense have struggled with over the last few months. And no doubt Rene himself. Theories and speculations suggested answers, but none proved conclusive, and the most likely explanation was some glitch in Rene's artificially grown brain, which was impossible to determine empirically without extraction and dissection. The critics have suggested it, even lobbied it in Congress, but were shut down. In the end, once Rene pleaded guilty, the answer to the question became immaterial.

I swallow before saying, "You will find this hard to believe, but I don't know. What's more, it bothers me just as much as it does you."

James nods. "You're right. I find it hard to believe."

I can only shrug. I'd like to say a lot here but can't. Of Rene, of Frankie Mason, of . . . but instead, I ask, "You two are graduating from UCSB in a few months, correct?"

James shifts his weight, crossing arms on his chest. "What of it?"

"When you are ready, I'd like to find the answer to your question together. I still have some pull with the Providence Foundation, and if you are looking for a job come spring . . ."

With a bemused smile, James rubs his eyelid with his middle finger. "You're serious, aren't you? Jesus fuck. Have a good life, Mr. Williams."

And then he walks off, still shaking his head as he disappears behind trimmed trees. Thomas, however, stands where he was, biting his lower lip and eyeing the folder in my hand.

I turn my attention to him and raise the folder with the Providence logo printed in gold. "We both know James doesn't need a job," I say, "but you might, Tom."

He looks me in the eye, his lips pressed into a fine line, and brushes a lock behind his ear. "Maybe."

"Definitely. I can do little to change what happened, but I can offer you and James support and even my friendship in the future. As soon as you graduate, it would be my honor to work with you up there on Peary-I." I hand him the folder. "No need to give your answer right now. You have a couple of months to think it over. Talk to James for me, will you?"

Tom shuts the folder. "I'll try, but I doubt he'll agree to this."

I smile. "He just might."

CHAPTER 6

It took the monorail twenty minutes to travel from the Orlando International Airport to the Cape Canaveral Spaceport, and Tom spent the time double-checking their tickets and making sure they had all the proper passes ready, tucked in a little pouch he wore across his chest.

"Let me see your UCSB pass," he said, nudging James.

"In my bag," James mumbled.

He'd spent most of their short flight from California asleep, and now, seated comfortably next to Tom, he had his arms crossed on the table, resting his forehead, his hair sprawled every which way. Tom reached down for the backpack and rummaged through it before producing a plastic ID card.

"I'll hold on to it for now."

"Do we even need them?"

"Yes." Tom left it at that and tucked the documents into his travel pouch that bore a NASA sticker they'd gotten at training.

Outside, endless fields and swamps painted a pretty but dull picture, and the Florida skies were overcast by a sheet of gray clouds that promised no rain. As Tom stared out the windows, mentally checking off the list of things they'd brought, he wondered what it would feel like to take off. Soon, they passed Port Canaveral, and the rail gently turned left along the coast.

The PA system dinged, crackled, and a prerecorded voice announced their arrival at the Spaceport in a few minutes.

"Come on, Jim, wakey-wakey."

James stirred and snapped upright, brushing back his hair and yawning. Tom handed him his headband with a little smile.

"Thanks." James put the band on, shook his head, and blinked.

"You ready?"

They were the first ones to get off the train and enter the main terminal of the Spaceport, where wide screens advertised the most popular attractions of Mars—rover tours, camping, and meditation chambers out in the plains. Images of blue sunsets succeeded those of majestic sand yachts and smiling families. In the ad, the moon was merely a way station on your journey to another planet. Few people around them paid the ads any attention, yet Tom beamed as they passed the screen on their way to check in.

After biometrics and a couple ID scans, they walked hand in hand, Tom mostly dragging James around, exploring the crowded main terminal. A hundred feet above their heads, hanging from the glass-and-steel ceiling, planes and rockets swayed on cables, all pieces of aeronautic history in their full glory. Tom's neck ached, and he dragged James to the tall windows overlooking the port. In the distance, mobile service towers lined the coast with a couple cargo rockets resting on their pads, supported by trusses, like giant mile markers measuring the coast. He counted at least a dozen towers and six rockets getting ready for launch. Closer to them, navigating the tarmac, slick silver shuttles taxied back and forth, and further north they rolled, lifted off, and climbed into the cloudy sky.

Tom fingered the glass. "That's the one we're taking, right?"

"*Hypervelocity*, yeah," James confirmed, nodding at a slim tri-engine shuttle reflecting the dreary sky.

"Come on, sweets, get excited!"

"I mean, it's a shuttle, Tom. I've seen shuttles before."

"Oh, have you, now?" Tom nudged him, bouncing from foot to foot. "Well, I haven't, and it's—"

James put an arm around him. "Exciting? Yeah, I guess so. Listen, how about I get something to drink, and we'll meet at the lounge?"

"Really? It's ten in the morning."

"Not on the moon it isn't," James said.

"Go ahead, then."

Tom kissed him, handed him his ID, and James walked off toward the food court with noticeable enthusiasm. Tom sighed. At least it gave him some time to swing by the gift shop. He waited a few more minutes, taking in the view, his heart beating faster in anticipation, and then headed for the shops.

His first stop was a small jewelry store on the corner—a kiosk really—all white and glistening with rings and pendants. It lacked the usual gift shop trinkets and thus lacked customers. The clerk greeted him as Tom approached the counter. Under the glass, colorful enamel pins rested in a grid of suede boxes, forming a rainbow of flowers of all shapes. There were too many to choose from, but Tom knew exactly what he was looking for.

"I don't really care for flowers," James had said when they first started going out.

Tom focused on the purple-blue section, searching for just the right one.

"But if you had to pick?" he had asked.

James had frowned at the bright orange tulip field around them, squinting from the sun. "Irises, I guess. These are too . . . toxic-looking."

Tom had only smiled, and now, he pointed at a fine blue-and-gold flower. The clerk nodded and took it out, and a minute later, Tom had it stashed in his bag and was walking out of the store.

His heels clicked on the floor, and his little suitcase rolled behind him as he made his way past the toy store and the various boutiques. With the pin safely hidden in its little box, Tom headed for the Space Center gift shop. Guarding the doors stood two spacemen, one in a classic bulky spacesuit from the dawn of space travel, the other in a modern one, thin and silvery, both sporting NASA insignias and golden helmets. Tom watched himself in the reflections as he went in, passing a rack of branded key chains and magnets.

Inside, Tom was assaulted by blue lights, glistening surfaces, and mountains of branded clothes, toys, and trinkets. In a far corner, next to a sturdy table of thick books, Tom found the spinning rack of postcards. Simple and cheesy, they made for the perfect present. He picked one and was about to head to the cashier when he spotted James out in the terminal.

"What the . . ." Tom muttered and ducked behind the rack, keeping the card close to his chest. He wouldn't have much time to put together a surprise up on the moon, and the last thing he wanted was to be caught with the card at the register.

He peeked out and saw James on the floor, looking around as if searching for someone. His headband was gone, and his hair flowed freely when he turned his head. His jumpsuit seemed to be stained, and his movements abrupt and disoriented. Was he searching for Tom? Why? He could've called. He might've gotten drunk already, but then he wouldn't be roaming the port—more like dozing somewhere in a corner booth. Maybe he was preparing a surprise of his own? Tom smiled at the thought and hid again to wait a few more minutes. When he popped up again, his partner was gone. Crisis averted.

They'd spent every day of the last few months together, whether at home or out in the city, and Tom had grown to cherish these little moments when he could walk about on his own—especially when it gave him time to get James a little present.

With the card in his bag next to the lapel pin, Tom went out and walked the floor, taking in the busy atmosphere of crowds about to embark on an interplanetary journey. Most of them would be going to Mars, many returning home from their summer vacations on Earth, some directly, some stopping for a layover, while others would stay on the moon for work. Tom's jaw hurt from smiling so much.

The food court met him with smells of junk food and coffee and screams of excited kids. He walked through the sitting area to the finer establishments hidden in the back behind wooden and glass doors in corners with subdued lighting. The Astra Lounge had the right vibe. Faux-leather armchairs and low tables peppered the space, occupied by serious-looking businessmen and women drinking from thin-stemmed glasses. No one paid him much attention as Tom crossed the room and landed on a bar stool next to James.

"Were you looking for me?" Tom said.

"When?"

"A few minutes ago, out in the terminal."

James turned to him, his fingers wrapped around a low-ball of mostly ice. Was it his second? Third? His hairband rested on the wooden bar next to the glass. "Why would I be looking for you? You know where I'm at."

Tom let out a heavy sigh. "I guess I do. Fine, be that way."

Tom considered ordering a drink of his own, but his stomach wouldn't handle it with all the excitement, and definitely not later, when the shuttle would be breaking the sonic barrier.

"What have you been up to, babe?" James said, finishing off his drink.

"Just window shopping. Is it cold on the moon?"

"Shouldn't be." James shrugged. "They have this complex atmosphere control system that keeps it all nice and cozy. My dad took me when I was a kid, back when they had the theme parks there . . ." He shook his head, staring at the drink in his hand.

Tom touched his knee. "We're almost there, okay? We should go."

James nodded and waved a hand over a terminal in the bar to pay. He grabbed the handle of Tom's suitcase, and they walked out of the lounge, back into the blinding daylight of the main terminal.

Half an hour later, the line at their gate finally moved, and the jetway brought them into the cabin of the shuttle *Hypervelocity*. The deep blue interior welcomed them with a smell of sandalwood, and the chairs were as sturdy as Tom had imagined—and hoped—they would be. They put the bags away and got situated in their seats, fixing the harnesses, while stewards ushered the other passengers.

Soon, an attendant walked the aisles and handed out their flight pills. Tom took his immediately and washed them down with some water.

"I'm good," James said. "I'd like to be present."

Tom couldn't help but smirk at that, and he would've added a remark as well, but then the pills kicked in, and that no longer mattered. His body relaxed, and his vision blurred slightly, and that was okay.

"Welcome aboard flight MP-111 headed for the Peary-I Armstrong Spaceport on . . . the moon!"

Someone behind them cheered, and the sound echoed in his head.

Sometime later, the shuttle rolled onto the runway, ignited the engines, and blasted off. Tom barely felt the extreme forces that pressed his body into the seat, focusing instead on the blurry world outside the windows. It was as if his mind drifted next to his relaxed body, receiving visual information but barely registering movement.

And then the world changed orientation, and suddenly the ground disappeared to his left as the shuttle began its vertical climb. They pierced the gray sheet of clouds and soon were leaving Earth behind.

CHAPTER 7

———

The moon snuck up on him. Tom opened his eyes, and there it was, out in the window—a static white sphere, brilliant against the black space, its darker mares cold and foreboding and unexplored. For now, at least.

The artificial gravity of the shuttle gently pushed him into the seat, and he unfastened the harness and wiggled out of it, gluing himself to the cold glass. A muffled hum of the engines filled the cabin, and though it was impossible to tell, the shuttle was moving, and the moon was slowly growing closer.

"This is incredible," Tom said under his breath.

"Yeah, cool view." Next to him, James knocked back a slender glass of red wine. Sprawled in his seat, he set the glass down and propped his chin on his left hand. "We're about half an hour out. Did you get some rest?"

Tom stretched and forced himself to turn away from the window. "Could use some more . . . and a shower. Did I sleep the whole time?"

James grinned. "Magic pills, huh? Here."

He handed Tom a teakwood tumbler of water, and Tom gulped it and asked for another.

"Space travel will do that to ya," James noted as he waved over a steward who was busy tending to other passengers.

Before long, they each had a new glass and watched the Peary-I Spaceport glisten in the distance. Located in the Peary crater close to the moon's north pole, the base stood out as a cluster of interconnected silvery-white domes. Tom couldn't quite make out any details yet, except for the silver web of landing strips that surrounded the Spaceport building to the right of the research base. At this distance, it still looked small, barely enough for a few people to inhabit, and it was hard to believe the facility housed upward of a thousand permanent residents.

Soon, he could see individual craft leaving the port and coming in for landing as well as smaller ground vehicles traveling to and from the base. Maintenance, he guessed, or maybe prospecting. The domes themselves were clearer now, with small windows and lights here and there. Some were as small as a baseball diamond, and others varied in size, all spread around the largest central dome that housed Peary Square. Between the domes and the tunnels that connected them, a sea of solar panels colored the ground a shimmering black.

"That's magnificent," Tom whispered, and James leaned over the armrest to take a peek.

"Welcome to our new home, eh?" He sniffed. "You really could use a shower, you know that?"

Tom grunted, but James snuck a kiss and plopped back into his seat. "It's gonna be fine, Tommy. I hear the facility's even got a public pool and a sauna." On the seats in front of them, a faint red light blinked, and they fastened the harnesses.

"Maybe we could hit those in the morning . . ."

A few minutes later, the harnesses locked, and the artificial gravity subsided. Tom pushed his feet into the bar in the footwell to fight the rapid deceleration. He squeezed James's hand and swallowed, getting ready for the landing. The shuttle pivoted and circled the crater, giving them another panoramic view of the Peary-I base, and descended toward the runway.

Thanks to the lack of gravity, they barely felt the touchdown, and when the moon's own field took over, Tom relaxed and let it pull him down.

"See? That wasn't so bad," James said as they rolled toward the main terminal, and he patted Tom's hand. "Aren't you excited?"

"No, I am, I am. Especially now that we're on solid ground. You?"

"I'm glad we're finally here," James said.

Tom didn't say anything and simply watched the Peary-I Spaceport lights flashing atop the terminal, welcoming travelers and visitors. The shuttle finally rolled to a stop.

Inside, the port wasn't as grand as the one back on Earth. The design choices had all been made decades prior, and while it had since been updated and decorated to give the port a more welcoming interior, the straight angles and flat walls betrayed its pragmatic origins. The facility started out as the Earth's first settlement on the moon, doubling as a research facility and a mining operation. In the decades since, it had grown to the size of a small town, yet as they picked up their baggage at the conveyor belt, all Tom could think of was how the astronauts must've felt during those first days of discovery.

"Impressed yet?" James said.

"Not really, to be honest."

And he wasn't. The wide space around them hardly differed from a regional airport on Earth except the windows here opened to a seemingly endless grid of tarmac beneath a black, starless sky.

"It gets better."

"Hope so," Tom said. "Which way?"

To their right, the terminal extended into the commercial part of the base, which housed a couple hotels, a shopping plaza, and attractions tourists could experience on their way to or from Mars. James grabbed Tom's hand, and they went left, headed toward the Providence Institute, past some planted trees and glass doors marked *Lounge* on their way to pass control. Ahead, a sign told them they were about to enter a restricted area.

"The blue corridor," Tom said, reading the small print on their tickets.

"Right."

They each passed through a biometrics cabin and scanned their IDs, and then further confirmed all the info with an immigration agent seated behind a low counter. She made sure everything was in order and gave them each a slim digital wristband to use at the base. Another short walk down a short corridor brought them to Peary Square.

"Welcome to Providence."

Tall double doors slid open, and they found themselves on a raised balcony above the square, and Tom froze.

"Now, I'm impressed."

Without waiting for James's reply, Tom walked over to the edge and leaned on the glass railing. The central dome that had seemed ambiguous in its size on their approach now filled his whole vision, so far above that it was difficult to judge the distance to the ceiling. Some twenty feet below, the square itself made him think of a mega mall—a vast pedestrian zone with a lively cafe in the middle surrounded by various businesses and two-story offices. Circling the square was a two-lane road, and small vehicles coursed around with occasional stops, letting passengers out and picking them up. Most people, though, preferred to walk.

"This is more like it, huh?" James said, leaning next to him. "I could see us living here. That cafe? And there's people sailboarding!"

"Look up, Tommy."

Tom did, at precisely the moment the dome opened up on the black sky, as if a giant eye was opening to darkness. A section of it showed the sky, still starless, with a single bright spot hanging in the middle—the Earth, a blue-and-white little circle.

Tom stared until his eyes teared up. "I can't believe this. It's real, right?"

"Oh, yeah. I mean, it's a projection, but it does show the world outside. Cool, huh?"

"It is. Hey, hold on . . ."

Tom walked from the railing to where James had left their suitcase in the middle of the balcony. Was this the right time? The trip had been exhausting, but how could they rest in this new, exciting world? Tom fished through his bag and found the pouch of brown paper he'd tucked away.

"What do you have there, sweets?" James said, still leaning on the glass railing but now half-turned.

"Just a little something to remember the moment by. Sorry it's not in a wrapper."

James took the pouch and inspected it. "It's perfect."

Tom's heart raced, and he couldn't stop smiling. He licked his lips. Sometimes, things could really be perfect, and maybe this would mark a new beginning for them. He glanced up at Earth and then back at his partner, but saw James was looking aside—something down at the square had caught his attention.

"Is that guy waving at us?" he asked.

Tom followed his gaze and, down below at the curb of the roundabout, saw a man standing next to a small ground vehicle, one hand in the air and waving. He wore a uniform of some kind, but it was hard to see any insignia, and the car itself had no marks other than a Peary-I logo on its door.

"He is, I think," Tom said. "Didn't know someone would be meeting us."

"Guess they are." James glanced down at the still-wrapped present, and then at Tom. "Let's save it till we get home, yeah?"

Tom frowned but nodded and tucked the pouch away. They grabbed their suitcases and took an escalator down to the plaza to what appeared to be a bus stop of sorts with a couple benches and a timetable on a stand. The man at the vehicle waved them over with a smile on his face.

"Mr. Mason, Mr. Brown-Allen. Let me grab your bags, guys!"

"We got it, thanks," James replied as Tom gave a weak wave. "They sent you for us?"

"They did, yes. The name's Deputy Bloom."

Tom shook his hand. Bloom gestured to the back of the car, and James popped the hatch open and loaded their baggage.

"Sorry about the mess," Bloom said. "I was given short notice."

"You're good." James shut the hatch. "Deputy, huh?

"Part-time." Bloom beamed. "You can call me Ray."

"I won't."

The three of them stood awkwardly for a moment, and Tom found himself in the middle of an unspoken conversation as James studied the deputy, who held his gaze. Suddenly, Bloom said, "We better get going."

Tom glanced back and forth between the two, and then said, "Yeah, let's do that."

He got in the back, looking out the window at the busy plaza, waiting for James to join him. People seemed to be enjoying their evening, walking around in pairs and groups, some with drinks and some with ice cream, as if they weren't walking on the moon at all. He could hardly imagine getting used to it this much. Perhaps with time.

Finally, James got in next to him, and Ray Bloom took control behind the wheel. The car hummed to life and took off, gliding clockwise around the square, the Luna Cafe on their right, and a series of stores and offices on their left.

Without music or conversation, the ride was almost eerie until James said, "So, Deputy Bloom, you said the sheriff sent you after us?"

Bloom glanced at them in the rearview mirror. "I didn't say that. But don't worry, no official business today. Just a ride."

"That's good," Tom said. And then, in a small voice, he added, "Just to clarify, you are taking us to our place, right?"

Bloom snorted. "Of course. Why would I be taking you anywhere else?" Behind the soft-spoken courtesy was an intensity that made Tom shiver. And then Bloom said, "Just messing with you. Not much policing to be done on Peary anyway. Actually, we all wear a couple hats up here. I run an éclair shop on the corner of three o'clock." He glanced at their confused faces in the mirror and said, "On the Peary Square here, those are the unofficial directions. Imagine a clock face, right? The Spaceport is six o'clock, and we're currently on the corner of nine."

Just then, they stopped at a crosswalk with a roundabout exit to their left—a tall one-lane tunnel with a monorail in the middle and a wide sidewalk on either side. The arch above the tunnel entrance glowed a subdued yellow and invited them to the Collins Residential Cluster.

Bloom said, "Twelve o'clock is where the main research facilities are located, and three is a . . . restricted area."

"Military?" James asked.

"Among other things."

Tom barely listened, instead watching a woman cross the road, giving Bloom a short wave and a smile, which the deputy returned. She went on toward the cafe, tapping at her wrist comm. They turned left and took the tunnel, and there was little conversation until they reached their destination a few minutes later.

Dome C7 welcomed them with a deep blue evening sky and gentle streetlamps along the street walled by three-story living quarters, a few dozen in total, built of steel and stone. Tom felt for James's hand and squeezed it lightly.

"And we'll be paid for living here?" he said.

Bloom glanced at them. "For working here, but yes, this will be your home for the duration of your contract."

They passed by windows emanating soft light, the interiors hidden behind closed blinds, and small strips of parking spaces with no more than a dozen small vehicles in total—it seemed personal transport wasn't a must around Peary-I. Every couple of buildings were separated by narrow alleys, and Tom stole a glance into cozy courtyards with benches and lawns.

Bloom drove them to the edge of the dome and stopped at the curb a few buildings away from a maintenance hangar that seemed to extend beyond the wall of the dome.

"Building seventeen," he said. "You need help with the bags?"

"We got it," James said as he stepped out.

Tom lingered behind a moment. "But thank you. We'll come by for those éclairs in the morning, if you don't mind."

"I'd love that, Mr. Brown-Allen. Welcome to the moon."

Tom's heart fluttered at the words.

They got the suitcases and watched Bloom turn around and whiz away the way they came, his taillights disappearing in the tunnel. Tom glanced up at the fake sky and breathed in the cool artificial air.

"Not too bad," James said.

They went down an alley, their steps clicking on the stone and echoing between the steel buildings, their shadows moving in odd directions as they passed underneath numerous lamps. Building seventeen stood adjacent to eighteen, the two of them mirror images of one another.

James swung the unlocked door open, and they found themselves in what would pass for a studio apartment back on Earth. A tight space but ergonomically furnished, its living room had a small kitchen and a wardrobe at the door with a sofa and an armchair in the living area. Tom noticed a narrow door that led into the courtyard as well. In the corner to their right, a set of wooden stairs led to the second floor and, presumably, their bedroom.

"Home sweet home."

James left the bags at the door and crashed on the sofa as Tom took a step in, his arms crossed. "Would now be a good time to talk about it?" he said.

"Your present?" James smiled, stretching out. "I'm ready."

"About why you really agreed to come to the moon."

CHAPTER 8

———

The staring match continued for a few long moments. Tom stood at the edge of the room, arms crossed. James lay on the sofa, one hand propping up his head, one hand drumming on his thigh. He said, "Can't we just celebrate the move tonight? Tell you what, I'll make drinks, and we can take it upstairs."

Tom stared for a long moment. "You're unbelievable. They just happened to send a cop to bring us here?"

James scoffed. "He's a deputy. And from where I'm standing, this was just a courtesy. I bet they do that for all new arrivals."

Thoughts raced through Tom's tired mind, mixed with curse words, accusations, and bizarre theories he could never articulate. Finally, he took his shot in the dark, saying, "Is he helping you in any way, Jim?"

James's lips parted, and then closed. He took a deep breath, then said, "Not everything is about that fucking robot, okay?"

"Isn't it?"

James sighed, sprawling on the sofa, his eyes glued to the ceiling. "Can't we just take it in tonight?"

"I guess we can't," Tom said, and he grabbed his backpack and headed upstairs. "I'm showering, and then I'm going to sleep. You're unpacking."

He only heard James grunt as he headed into the bathroom on the second floor.

They woke up six hours later to the sounds of birds chirping as sunlight pushed through the blinds. Both were artificial, but it took Tom a moment to realize and dismiss. James's arm was wrapped around his chest, and Tom patted it lightly before turning. James had crawled into bed late last night, whispering a "sorry," and Tom had mumbled something noncommittal in response. Technically, they'd not gone to bed angry.

"Morning," James said.

"Hey."

"Ready to take on the day?"

Tom's wristband vibrated lightly. "Someone's at the door," he said, "ringing the bell."

"You go."

Tom rolled out of bed and got into his last night's clothes— James, of course, had not unpacked—and went downstairs, shoving suitcases out of the way before opening the door. He half-expected it to be Bloom out there, bright and early with inspection, and had some words ready . . . but no such luck.

"Good morning!" A woman beamed at him. She wore a green-and-white jumpsuit with a Peary-I logo on her chest and her curly black hair in a messy bun. "I'm Adelia. Adelia Farewell. You're new here, right?"

"We are. And yeah, morning to you too. I'm Tom."

She shook his hand. "Nice to meet you, neighbor! I'm over there in building seven." She motioned somewhere behind her. "Apartment B. It's your first day, right?"

Her eyes glowed with excitement that Tom found hard to match at this early hour. He suppressed a yawn and said, "It is going to be, yeah." Was that too harsh? He added a smile, just in case.

"Exciting! So much for you to see around here! You will love the research facility! What department are you in?"

Tom blinked, and then invited her in. "Coffee?"

"Would love some!" Adelia stepped through and headed for the tiny kitchen island, where she hopped on one of the two stools. She inspected the immaculate kitchen, drumming her hands on the table.

Tom said, "I don't know how to work this yet, so . . ."

"Oh, no problem! I got you!" She smiled and circled the island to put on the coffee machine. "These condos are all the same, you know."

"Makes sense. Um . . . Give me five?"

Tom's hand was on the handle of a large suitcase. Adelia glanced at it, and then back at him. "Oh, go ahead, I've got this."

Tom offered a small smile and lugged the bag upstairs, banging it on each step. Dropping it off in the bedroom, he knocked on the bathroom door, where James was taking a shower. "We've got guests, so you better come down."

No reply came, so Tom opened the suitcase and changed into a pair of pants and a long-sleeved shirt and then put on his green-and-white uniform. Despite the brightness of the new day, the dome had a constant temperature, which was just below comfortable, so he opted to throw on a long coat as well.

Downstairs, Adelia waited on a stool, and three cups of coffee steamed in front of her. "Cream? Sugar?"

"Yes to both," Tom said as he joined her. "So, Adelia, right?" She nodded. "What do you do up here?"

"Oh, a bit of this, a bit of that. I'm a communications officer, a department liaison at the facility. Everything to do with bringing people together, really. Wearing many hats around here. We have an annual short play competition coming up, if you're interested." He shrugged, so she sipped her coffee. "What about you, Tom?"

"I'm a civil engineer. Building roads on Mars and all that. Well, not literally, obviously, but potentially. Maybe in a few years . . ."

Adelia nodded to every word, holding her cup next to her lips.

Tom had to admit, her energy was invigorating. Or maybe it was the caffeine. Either way, he said, "Did you know the projects we're working on here are being actually built on Mars? I mean, yeah, they tested it here on Peary initially, but all Martian infrastructure gets developed here and then implemented on the spot. Guess it's cheaper that way."

"That's by design, too," Adelia said. "Providence has the contracts to ensure Mars doesn't go too independent. It's a whole political power play thing, from what I've heard. Roads, though, huh? That's exciting, right?"

Tom shrugged. "I think so. But roads are only a part of it. It's the domes, the railways, the spaceports . . . it's quite magical, really. We take a barren, cold wasteland and turn it into a city for a thousand people or more! Out of nothing!"

Adelia said, "Now if you could just take care of terraforming, then we could even enjoy the sun for real!"

Tom snickered and sipped his coffee. "That's the next step, I'm sure. A lot of quirks to figure out before you can turn rocks into a paradise."

"Sure smells like paradise in here," James said as he strode down to join them. "Who have we here? Hi!"

They made introductions, and James climbed onto the stool next to Adelia and told her all about his applied physics work back at UCSB and how harnessing the power of the sun was humanity's ticket out of the solar system. Tom, in turn, wanted to get out of the house.

"Breakfast?" he said.

"Yeah," James agreed. "Bloom's?"

Tom narrowed his eyes. "Sure, éclairs sound great."

Adelia emptied her cup and gathered theirs to put them away. "Our dishwashers are small, but they do the job," she noted. "By the way, you guys need a ride?"

A few minutes later, they climbed into Adelia's little car—identical to Bloom's—and she took them to the Peary Square. In the morning, if it could be called that, the square bustled with people. Joggers were out on their first run of the day. Couples relaxed on numerous benches. Even more people darted back and forth, most of them wearing the green-and-white uniforms. Most stores along the dome's wall were open, and Tom noticed more cafes and restaurants.

Adelia took them counterclockwise around the square, and they parked near the corner of three o'clock. "Bloom's Éclairs," she announced.

James opened the door and said, "You're not coming?"

"I do have a job to go to." She offered an apologetic smile. "I'll see you guys around, yeah?"

"Have a stellar day," Tom said, and immediately regretted doing so—it sounded better in his head.

"Oh, also," James said, "what's a good place to have dinner?"

"The Needle," she replied. "It's usually light on traffic at the end of the day."

"Good to know. Farewell, Adelia Farewell." James patted the roof.

Adelia giggled and waved, and she took off as soon as they were on the sidewalk.

"She's fun, isn't she?" James said.

Tom and James stood for a moment, watching her circle the square and disappear into the twelve o'clock tunnel. The central dome's ceiling was projecting the outside as the night before, but there was no imitation of a blue sky, only the same blackness of space and ethereal light. Tom turned his face up but felt no warmth.

Bloom's éclair shop, as promised, was located on the corner of the Peary Loop and three o'clock in a steel outbuilding, as if converted from an Airstream trailer. In the front, below a pale neon sign, a blue-and-pink canopy sheltered a few bistro tables.

"Why are we here?"

"Éclairs, Tommy. Why else?"

Inside, Deputy Bloom himself was working the conveyor, dressed in a green-and-white jumpsuit with its sleeves rolled up and an apron the same colors as the canopy. It seemed to be a busy morning, with boxes of fresh éclairs piling up on the counter and a few people waiting in line to pick up theirs from a large open window.

They joined the line, and all the while they waited, Tom stared at Bloom, trying to glimpse some kind of tell—a tick or a nervous glance toward them. Neither manifested, and the closer they came to the guy, the more ridiculous Tom's suspicions sounded in his head. Why would a Peary deputy be helping James in some kind of plot to find Rene? If there even was a plot.

"Half a dozen glazed ones," James said.

Bloom whipped around. In this new context, the man looked . . . happier. His face was brighter, and the smile was sincere. Still, Tom picked up on the pause—a bit longer than the situation called for.

"What flavor?" Bloom said. "I just made these white chocolate strawberry ones."

Tom glanced at the display and his mouth watered. The éclairs glistened in the sun, and some were even still steaming.

"At least three of those," he said.

"And coffee, if you make it."

"To go?"

"No," James said, "we're staying."

Again, an odd moment passed between the two of them, and Tom wanted nothing more than to get away from the place. Well, except maybe the éclairs. After the briefest pause, Bloom only nodded, and James stepped away, stopping at a table nearby. Tom was behind him.

"What was that about? What's going on?"

James studied his face, and then said, "We've been over this, babe, and no, I'm not in cahoots with Deputy Bloom to track down and kill Rene Robertson in an act of revenge. I'd just like to get a bite. Does that fully answer it?"

Tom breathed. He wanted to believe it, but . . . "Then what are those weird looks you keep giving the guy? If that's your new way of flirting . . ."

James grinned. "I wish. Listen, Tommy, they know who we are, right? I mean, they have to know. They know who I am, more specifically. You said it last night, and I agree with you—they didn't just happen to send a cop to pick us up."

Tom didn't see why they wouldn't—he wanted to believe it really had been just a courtesy. Bloom ran a pastry shop and drove a little golf cart. Surely it wasn't that big a deal.

"It was a message," James said. "They're saying, 'We're watching you, kid, so you better not get any ideas.'"

That made sense. It had been the case of the century, and both he and James—James more so—had become celebrities of sorts. Rene Robertson was the first sentient android to not only kill a human, but, in many people's opinions, to practically get away with it. While the trial lasted, James had been often asked whether he planned to take matters into his own hands, but he'd always replied that revenge wasn't on his mind. Looking into his partner's eyes now, Tom wasn't so sure. He spoke with subdued spite, as if holding himself back from letting his real thoughts slip.

"And what's the message you're sending back?" Tom said.

"That I'm not scared of them."

Tom rolled his eyes. "Seriously?" And then he caught himself. "Why would that be a concern?"

"It's not, but they need to know we don't need extra supervision, right? We're here to do the job." He put his hand on Tom's and added, "I just want this to be a new beginning for us."

James's hand was warm and a little dry—Tom made a mental note to make him use lotion later—but most of all, it was reassuring. Maybe, just maybe, this was the opportunity he'd been looking for. A chance to get away and start anew, somewhere where nobody cared about—

"Six glazed and two coffees!" Bloom yelled.

—still, Rene Robertson was out there. Somewhere on this base, doing whatever androids were good for. Accounting? Admin? He imagined the robot tucked away in some dark backroom or basement where his identity wouldn't matter. What were the chances of them ever meeting?

"You ready?" James said, handing him a bamboo cup and a paper tray with three strawberry éclairs on it.

"Where to?"

"For a walk, but there might be a surprise in it for you later on." James winked as he brought up a hologram of the facility map, and they agreed on a route. They strolled down the promenade, across the road, and toward the twelve o'clock tunnel where their work would start tomorrow.

CHAPTER 9

——

It took them a couple hours to circle Peary Square. They consumed the pastries on a nearby bench, watching a small statue of an hourglass spinning at the center of a gyroscope. No plaque explained it, but it was mesmerizing nonetheless. After breakfast, James dragged Tom into a screening of an old disaster flick that James unapologetically loved—and then Tom dragged him to the recreation dome to play a game of badminton that James hated. On the whole, the day was a success.

In the evening, they scouted the few shops, most of which were carbon copies of retail chain locations from Earth with little variation in product—clothes, shoes, office supplies. The only thing Peary seemed to have an abundance of were books. The multinational population of the facility meant that the many shelves of the local two-story bookstore were lined with books in a dozen languages on every topic imaginable, all primed to take away the inhabitants' boredom.

Tom flipped the pages of one with a monk and a castle on the cover, enunciating its Italian title.

"You better give up, sweets," James teased, peeking over his shoulder. He scanned the page. "Love and meaning? What a drag."

"And naps, I think." Tom shut the book and half-turned. "I think you'd like this one, actually. Maybe learn a thing or two? At least we both need to learn Italian, at some point. You know, for when we travel, back on Earth."

"Europe?" James said, planting his chin on Tom's shoulder. "You're standing on the moon and you wanna go to Europe?"

"I'm buying it." Tom scanned the softcover with his wristband and tucked it into his hip bag. As they headed out, he said, "Hey." James stopped. "Sorry about the morning, okay? I was grumpy, jet lagged. I overreacted."

James smiled and took his hand. "All good. I know this whole thing is a lot to take in. It's a big change, but one we've needed, yeah?"

Tom wanted to believe that, so he let James take him out of the store and down toward six o'clock, past more stores and the ticket center on their right. The street, as Tom came to think of it, was empty in this part of Peary, with only rare ground vehicles passing by on the narrow road to their left and a couple people on their evening walks. Strangers greeted them with smiles and nods, and Tom and James returned them.

"Are we leaving already?" Tom said. They passed by the escalators up to the Spaceport and then the bus stop where Bloom had picked them up.

"Not just yet. Hungry?"

Hidden in an alcove below the wide balcony, the entrance to The Needle whispered muffled music through a set of bright blue doors.

"I've booked a table," James said, and gestured for Tom to go on.

The doors slid open, and they walked down a short ramp that ended in a stone lobby with two elevators. Between them, seated behind a podium, a young woman beckoned them. "Welcome, you two. Oh, you're new! Swell!"

With a swift motion, she flipped the top of the stand, and James scanned his wristband. Once the info checked out, the hostess said, "You are in for a treat! The Needle is the highest point on the moon, both figuratively and literally!"

Tom raised a brow and reflexively glanced up at the ceiling. If he understood correctly, nothing but the Spaceport balcony was above them, and maybe a system of vents in the thick roof of the building.

"You guys on lunch break?" she said.

"We just got here."

"Must be tired from the flight, then? No matter, because The Needle will leave you both relaxed and entertained. Enjoy!"

She hit a button, and the elevator doors opened. They found themselves in a spacious rectangular room almost as big as their condo, with floor-to-ceiling windows that showed nothing and a metal bench in the middle with seats on both sides.

The hostess said, "Take a seat, relax, and enjoy the experience."

They did just that, facing the blackness, hand in hand. The doors closed without a sound.

"Is this a restaurant, or—"

"Shhh."

Orchestral music swelled, and a voice made to sound like radio chatter began a countdown. When it reached *one*, Tom could swear the elevator shot up, the gravity pushing him into the bench harder as the view in front of them changed. Darkness remained, but it was now the bottomless darkness of space with distant stars to their right where the moon was covered in shadow and the sun to their left where the elevator doors had been.

Laid out below them like a diorama, the Peary-I base sprawled in every direction, filling the crater, its domes giving off brilliant white light. Was it sparkling? Maybe. It took Tom a moment to orient himself, and then he realized they were looking at the research facilities—twelve o'clock—with the Spaceport behind them, living domes on their left, and the military installation—its gray domes just a shade lighter than the surface—on the right.

A moment later, he saw Earth up in the sky, that same blue-and-white light, surreal from this perspective.

"Where . . . where the hell are we going?" Tom said.

The elevator kept going up until they were what must've been hundreds of feet above the base. Beyond it, the cold and gray surface of the moon, peppered with craters and ranges, disappeared on the black horizon. Finally, they slowed almost to a stop, and then a set of doors appeared to their left. Tom got up and took a shy step to the windows. James joined, his eyes wide and his smile wider.

"What a view," he said, and then turned to Tom.

"Yeah . . . we're not floating in space, are we?"

"Well, in the grand scheme of things . . ."

Tom put his hand on the window and squinted, focusing his eyes on the glass, looking for the screen beyond it and not finding one.

The doors opened, and they stepped into The Needle. A lounge bar more than a restaurant, the interior mimicked the smoking parlors of old with dark wooden paneling on the walls and armchairs and sofas of green faux leather. Heavy curtains hid more digital screens, and the dim lighting paired with quiet music made Tom feel underdressed for the occasion. The patrons, groups of two and three, sat around low tables, talking and drinking, some eating canapés off little wooden trays.

Tom and James moved through the music-filled room, looking around like the newcomers they were.

"Oh, there she is," James said, and he pulled Tom after him across the room.

"There's who?"

And then he saw, seated in a corner booth, nursing a small flute of maroon liquid—Adelia Farewell. She wore a muted yellow dress with a small hat that hid her bun and shiny hoops in her ears. On the small table in front of her, a slim bottle and two additional glasses awaited. She saluted as they approached.

"Looking good in those overalls, boys, if not entirely festive!"

James got the chair for Tom. "We came straight from our tour around the facility."

"Port?" Adelia asked as she filled the glasses. "The Needle's got the best booze on the moon."

"Thanks," Tom said, and he emptied his in one gulp. He had a feeling he'd need it. The drink was cold and heavy with a sweet aftertaste. "Fancy meeting you here, Adelia."

She smiled. "Likewise, Tom, likewise. How did you find the station?"

"It's a lot more . . . familiar than I'd expected," he said.

"Yeah, they did a good job making us comfortable up here. There's a pond in the Japanese garden in Dome 9. I'll show you some time."

James raised his glass. "To our new home."

They clinked, drank, and Tom refilled. He eyed Adelia as she took a tiny sip of her drink. She caught his expectant stare and held it for a long moment, and then glanced at James. "So," she said, "in the end, it wasn't too hard . . ."

James gave her a look of feigned surprise.

Tom scoffed. "See, J? It wasn't too hard."

Adelia cleared her throat. "Am I missing something, guys?"

James pursed his lips and shook his head, and then drank some of his port. Adelia looked between them.

Tom sat back in his chair, feeling the alcohol relaxing his limbs already. He crossed his arms and said, "What is it that you found out, exactly?"

"Um, okay . . ."

Tom picked up his glass and took a sip.

"Would you slow down?" James said.

"Oh, don't you worry, this is my last one. Please, Adelia, continue."

Her brows shot up, and she took a breath before saying, "I found your Rene Robertson. It's not a big secret around here. He's sort of a celebrity, actually." She caught herself. "Sorry, I didn't mean to—"

"You're good, love," Tom said, twirling his free hand. "Carry on. James is all ears."

And he was. Despite Adelia's growing discomfort, James sat with his elbows on his knees, his fingers laced around his barely touched glass. "Go on," he said.

Adelia glanced at Tom but spoke to James. "He works in three o'clock, as you suspected, out in the mining facilities beyond the crater. Not exactly sure where. Anyway, he's got six-day shifts, and then he's back on the base for a day."

James nodded, no doubt taking mental notes while Tom finished his drink. He was about done.

"Do you have any pointers on where he goes?" James said. It was just him and his little spy now. He stared into the woman's eyes with singular intensity.

"My source"—she lowered her voice for effect—"tells me Mr. Robertson rarely leaves three o'clock, but they've seen him walk the square once."

"Why?"

Tom set his glass on the table. "Why the fuck do you think? People take walks."

Adelia leaned back, suddenly more interested in her drink.

James glared at Tom. "He's not a person."

Tom had heard all he needed to. Without a reply, he got up and left, walking straight for the elevators. He stared at the doors, tapping his foot, considering looking for the emergency stairs, when it dinged. The elevator's artificial gravity on the "way down" was only slightly lower, moving slower than it had on the "way up," and Tom couldn't be more grateful for that. He barely held the port wine down as he exited the doors, thanking the hostess for the experience.

"Have a great night, sir!"

Unlikely. Tom walked home the way they'd come, circling the square and turning into the nine o'clock tunnel. The strip of sidewalk, barely wide enough for three people, was empty at this hour, and he walked in the middle, glancing to his left every now and then through the only real windows on the station at the black sky.

"Tommy!"

He stopped, staring out toward the dim light at the end of the tunnel, where it turned into their residential dome. He waited.

James ran up behind him. "Will you look at me, at least?"

Tom turned, arms crossed on his chest. He bit his lips, not sure what to make of his feelings.

"I'm sorry, okay?" James said. "I shouldn't have lied."

Tom took a deep breath, and the cool air somewhat helped tame the port buzz. "Anything else you shouldn't have done?"

"Look, I know what you want me to say—"

"Yeah. Are you gonna?" He felt his throat go sore and his eyes get wet.

"No. I lied, yes, but you knew, didn't you? You didn't want to admit it to yourself, but you knew why I came here."

Tom swallowed. Wiped his cheek. "'Did you miss the part where you brought *me* along? You brought me to the fucking moon, and all to do what, exactly?"

James tucked his hands into the pockets of his jumpsuit. "I'm going after Rene Robertson."

"To do what?"

He shrugged. "Don't know yet."

Tom shook his head, looking into his partner's eyes, searching for . . . what? Regret? A plea? He found neither, at any rate. James was as resolved as ever, and now that he'd been caught, Tom knew, he'd only double down on his plan. Still, he had to try. "Don't," he said, putting his hands on James's shoulders. "Let's go home, get some sleep—"

He shook off Tom's hands and took a step back. "Adelia's waiting on me. Come along, Tommy. You haven't eaten."

"I've had enough."

Tom turned away and walked, ignoring the remarks James threw after him, focused only on that light in the distance. A shower, a warm bed, and work tomorrow.

CHAPTER 10

———

The next morning, Tom had to face the consequences of refusing the dinner. He'd dined on trail mix the night before—the only snack stocked in the kitchen cupboard—so he woke up early in the morning still hungover and groggy, his stomach rumbling. But it was his first day, so he dragged himself to the shower and then, not five minutes later, down into the kitchen, where he chugged three glasses of water.

James hadn't returned the night before, and Tom had to push down the worry to focus on the job. He went upstairs and dressed in his work uniform—a light blue jumpsuit and a jacket of the same color with his name embroidered on the chest. What else did he need? He'd packed his hip bag last night with all the materials he'd require in the office, and the wristband served as his pass.

The condo locked when he left and circled it to find a small compartment in the wall, which let out a beep and popped open when Tom swung his wrist next to it. He pulled out a compact scooter, unfolded it, and was on his way down the main tunnel.

The morning air wasn't much different from the evening air on Peary, and the view out of the thick tunnel windows hadn't changed—the same black space and gray landscapes in the distance. No more than half a dozen cars traveled the tunnels with him, but they joined a longer line as they neared the square. Tom whizzed and dodged between them, overtaking the carpoolers and turning left, headed for twelve o'clock. The Luna Cafe on his right was bustling with morning commuters grabbing a last-minute breakfast, but Tom decided not to risk it. As his mom would say, "On time is fifteen minutes early." So he waited for pedestrians to cross and took another left turn, entering the research part of the base.

Providence Foundation was written in shiny letters on a plaque above the entrance, which Tom found to be surprisingly minimalist. Instead of a checkpoint, two waist-high poles stood in the middle of the road with scuffed pads, where workers had to scan their bracelets. Tom did just that and rolled on, looking for his station.

The second turn on the right brought him to Engineering Dome 1, and Tom had to pump the breaks as he entered it, skidding slightly and coming to a stop at the curb.

"Whoa."

Unlike the residential dome, built to resemble a quiet neighborhood of townhouses, this one was built up to the ceiling two hundred feet overhead. A six-story building was essentially crammed into the space with some overhead tunnels and walkways connecting two halves of it. The strip of the dome ceiling he could see above ran parallel to the street and projected blue skies, and for a moment Tom found himself standing in a street of New York, staring up at the dark, uniform buildings that walled it. The building itself, like the one they lived in, was made of stone, glass, and metal, resembling any office building on Earth.

His neck was beginning to get sore, so Tom snapped back to reality and accelerated down the street to leave the scooter at a charging lot, and then went in through sliding doors.

"Thomas Brown-Allen," he said as he scanned his wristband at the desk in the lobby. The room was smaller than he'd have guessed, with only a front desk and two benches. In the middle of it, a tacky blue hologram of the engineering building slowly rotated.

"Good morning, Thomas," the woman behind the desk said. "Someone will come get you shortly. Please sit."

"Oh, okay."

He did, feeling the cold metal of the bench through his uniform. The hologram in front of him showed his future office without the dome—an awkward stack of angular buildings shimmering in the sun with its main street spreading in a web and connecting with surrounding sectors. Tom guessed the presentation was a leftover from at least a decade or two back, when hopes of terraforming the moon were still high, before those dreams shifted to Mars. Had they gone through with it then, Peary would've made for a fine moon town. Alas, Mars had proven to be more viable—and spacious—in the long term, so the moon base was destined to remain a research lab and transit station.

And now, Tom was sitting on a bench, about to go into work on a superhighway project being built on the red planet almost fifty million miles away. A sudden wave of anxiety hit him as more time passed. Suddenly, the whole facility felt too small, like a closet tucked away in the back where he was contracted to do grunt work for others. Tom's stomach complained and his head felt heavy, and he wished he'd stopped at Luna on his way over.

He spoke into his bracelet: "Ask James where the hell he is."

The comm dinged, and Tom waited for a reply. It'd been fifteen minutes since he'd showed up, and at one minute after eight in the morning, another set of doors slid open, and a gruff-looking man in his forties stepped into the lobby room. He was clean-shaven with his salt-and-pepper hair in a bun.

"You Thomas?" he asked, giving Tom a once-over.

"Yes, sir." Tom shot to his feet.

"Let's get you started, then."

They walked through the doors his supervisor had just emerged from and down a narrow hallway, its walls sparsely decorated with paper and digital posters touting the Providence team as the engineering elite—"Light-Years Ahead!" one said, "Moon and Beyond!" said another—with graphics and photos of the facility. Tom winced.

"I'm Sang, project admin around here. You won't be seeing me much, but I'll introduce you to the team." They walked for a moment before he asked, "What you gonna do besides build roads, Thomas?"

"You mean, in life?"

"I mean here. Like, what's your passion?"

He hadn't thought of that. With everything happening lately, exploring his passions seemed . . . frivolous. He wanted to mention sailboarding, but would that qualify as a passion? He said, "We'll see. One step at a time, I guess."

"Far out, Thomas." Sang pushed a door open, and Tom froze for a moment in the doorway. They entered a sprawling, open-plan space set twenty feet below ground level. Stand-up desks and chairs surrounded the empty area in the middle, and a few people had already taken position at their stations. Some were staring into an array of monitors while others manipulated holographic models. Perhaps the grunt work wouldn't be so bad after all.

"What do you think?"

"We had a similar setup at UCSB," Tom said, "but not on this scale. That's the simulation floor, right?"

"Yup." Sang nodded. "Everything we're working on gets integrated into the superhighway model and runs through constant simulations. Sixteen thousand a second, to be precise. They need this track to reach far and wide and to last a thousand years."

"I bet they want it on a budget, too?"

Sang chuckled. "You'll fit right in, Thomas."

"Should we go down there?" Tom asked, rolling on the balls of his feet.

"After you, kid."

Tom took a few steps toward the stairs, already eyeing his station and the gear he'd be using when Sang said, "Hold on a sec, Thomas."

Tom turned to see the admin reading something off his wristband, frowning. "What's up?"

"Odd. There's someone outside to see you."

Tom felt his face turn red. If James was going to apologize, he chose a terrible moment to do so. "Sir?"

"You should go see what's wrong, kid." Sang shrugged. "A slow day around here, anyway."

Tom offered a smile, and the guy returned it, and his laid-back attitude allowed Tom to relax a bit in turn. He nodded and went past his new boss. "Thanks."

"Don't forget to come back!"

"I won't be a minute."

He fast-stepped down the hallway, wringing his wrists and cracking fingers. What to say? *James, you need to go. I got no time for this today.* When had that ever worked? When J had his mind set on something, he would hear no objections. Tom could only hope there wouldn't be a scene.

But as he stepped through sliding doors into the front office, he didn't see his partner anywhere. Instead, another familiar face greeted him from the other side of the hologram. Tom walked over.

"Hey, Mr. Bloom, what brings you here?"

The man frowned. "You need to come with me, Mr. Brown-Allen."

Tom's heart sank. It didn't take a genius to figure out something had gone wrong, and he had a pretty good idea what.

Without further debate, he followed Bloom outside and to his small vehicle, which presented cleaner today and smelled of fresh éclairs and coffee. As they walked, Tom sent a message to his boss, saying he'd probably be late after all.

"How bad is it?" Tom said from the passenger seat as they left the engineering dome.

The deputy held a pause before saying, "I'll let the sheriff explain the situation. All I can tell you, Thomas, is that you need to pay close attention to what's about to happen."

Tom swallowed. *The sheriff. Jesus.* At the square, they turned left, and not right, which somehow made things worse—they weren't going home. A minute later, Bloom took another left turn, into the three o'clock tunnel. The military base. Unlike the other two tunnels Tom had been to, this one was protected by a set of metal doors that blocked the entrance, and a bright yellow stripe across them marked it as a restricted area. A bunch of flags and logos were painted below it, as well as a more thorough disclaimer in a small font.

Thankfully, they never reached the doors. Bloom turned right some forty feet away, into a bay hidden between the square and the entrance. They parked in a row of identical vehicles and walked over to the Peary Security Station—a small building designed like their townhouse. So far, so familiar. Tom had bailed out James a few times back on Earth, twice after anti-robot protests and twice after bar fights, so this part he knew all too well. Bloom led him up the few steps and invited him to go in.

The familiarity continued inside the station, sparsely furnished but lived-in and homely—photographs were on the walls and a thin beige carpet was on the floor, and the woman at the desk gave him a smile. Tom nodded in response. She invited him to what he thought would be the sheriff's office at the far end of the room, but the door he knocked on had no name plate next to it.

"There he is," Sheriff Greene cheered, standing at a . . . waist-high flower bed in the middle of a small greenhouse. Now that was new. He was a man in his late sixties with a full head of silver hair and a trimmed mustache to match it. He wore a gray jumpsuit with a black windbreaker over it and held a small pink rose in a gloved hand.

"Hey, Tom," James said from a corner, sitting in one of two metal chairs at the door. He looked pale and tired, even more so in the white LED light, struggling to keep his eyes open.

"Good morning, Sheriff," Tom said, covertly studying the space. He'd stayed by the closed door, arms crossed. "How can I help?"

Greene smiled. "Please sit down, Mr. Brown-Allen."

Tom lingered a moment but then took a seat next to James. The sheriff studied both of them, his brows and lips moving, and then he let the roses be and stepped around the flower bed. A certain joy was in his expression.

Not much policing to be done on Peary, Bloom had said, and perhaps this was Greene's rare moment to savor.

Finally, keeping eye contact with Tom, he said, "I'll say this once, boys, so listen closely. I know who you are, and I know why you're here. What's more, I knew this would happen the moment your names came across my desk six months back."

Six months? They hadn't even gotten the job offer until three months ago. Tom's face twitched.

"However," Greene continued, "this doesn't mean I'll stand for you running around the base on some cockamamie revenge mission. This is the moon, not Earth, and whatever happened there? Well, we prefer not to live in the past."

Tom glanced at James, who was focused on his shoes.

"This is all to say, boys, that you're getting a pass this one time. But if Deputy Bloom or I catch you as much as looking at three o'clock, I'll have to write up a report to send you home. Capeesh?"

"Yes, sir," Tom said. "Won't happen again. Right?"

All eyes were on James, and he nodded weakly. "Yeah. Maybe I'll pick up a different hobby here. Gardening?"

Tom said, "He promises, Sheriff. He's just—"

"Like I said, I know who you are and what you went through. I'm sorry about all that. But I hope we have an understanding. You've been here what, two days? Not even that?" Greene paused, and Tom waited. "I suggest the two of you take a closer look at your priorities today, yes?"

"Yes, sir."

Greene clapped his hands. "That's what I like to hear. Now then, I'll see you around, boys. Hopefully under nicer circumstances. Go on, then. I believe you've got jobs to get to."

Tom took James's hand and dragged him out of the greenhouse. Deputy Bloom waited for them out in the lot, seated in his vehicle with the door open, bobbing his head to some tune.

"Stop," James said, and he pulled Tom's hand.

"Can we do this after work?"

"No. Look, thank you for coming."

"Like I had a choice."

"Fair. Still."

"What did you do, James?"

He shrugged. "Doesn't matter now, because I'll need your help with what comes next."

Tom sighed. "Did you not hear the sheriff?"

A wide grin softened James's face, and he put a finger under his nose, imitating a mustache. In a low voice, he said, "Behave, you boys, or you'll go to moon jail!"

"Stop it," Tom said, but the corners of his lips twitched. "Seriously, what are you so happy about?"

James took his hand, lacing their fingers, and led him to Bloom's car. "I know where Rene Robertson is and, more importantly, I know where he is going to be four days from now."

CHAPTER 11

———

"Welcome aboard, Dr. Williams," Captain Byrnes says as I ascend the ramp and enter the shuttle *Narwhal Cargo* idling at Cape Canaveral Spaceport. He sits in one of the two pilot seats, dressed in an orange flight suit.

"Thank you, Captain. I hope I won't be too much of a nuisance during the flight."

"Not at all! After so many trips on this route, it's nice to see a fresh face."

I've taken the place of Byrnes's partner on this particular occasion. Not an ideal solution, but I had to make this trip without any extra attention, and this was the only available flight.

The crew cabin is tight but accommodating with a couple sleeping units, a bathroom, a kitchenette in the back, a common area, and two pilot seats in the front. The space is well used, too—the narrow metal countertop is scuffed, and the linens strapped to the beds are faded and bear cartoon characters. I tuck my carry-on into a storage compartment overhead and strap in. Byrnes studies the instruments on the many displays, and then we each press a start button, signaling to the tower that we're ready for takeoff.

"What are we hauling today, Captain?" I ask.

"Medical supplies, sir," the man says as the shuttle moves. We taxi to the runway on autopilot and watch the port ahead, glowing and alive. In the distance, commercial shuttles take off and land in the field of lights lining the tarmac. The engines whirl behind us, and the shuttle speeds up some.

"Narwhal-3, you are clear for takeoff."

I pop a flight pill. "Godspeed," I say under my breath and, out of the corner of my eye, see Byrnes's lips curve in a smile.

We pick up speed until our bodies press into the seats, and then we shoot up in the air. Blissfully, I drift off.

I come to a few hours later. The shuttle's artificial gravity pushes me into the seat, a little lighter than it would've been back on the ground. Captain Byrnes is still asleep next to me. Most displays are dark, except a couple right in front of us, tracking flight statistics—time, distance to our destination, and more. I undo the straps to go use the bathroom, comforted by the steady hum of the engines.

I return to find Byrnes awake and staring into the darkness in front of us with the moon's jewel in the middle of the viewscreen surrounded by smaller, dimmer lights.

"Lunch?" I call from the kitchenette.

"With a mango fresh, please, Dr. Williams."

"You can call me Haywood," I say, and I fish two lunch boxes out of the fridge and a packet of juice. "Say, Captain, how do you usually entertain yourself during these flights?"

As he talks, I use the moment to spike his juice by dropping in a capsule similar in composition to our flight pills, only stronger. "—and Pete usually hangs out in virtual, anyway, so not much conversation there."

I hand him the food and climb into my seat. "Can't call myself a chatterbox either, I'm afraid."

Byrnes chuckles. "That's quite alright, Haywood. I imagine this is a business trip for you? If you don't mind my asking."

He opens his lunch, taking a swig of the juice, and I give a short nod. "Always business when it comes to me and the moon."

Peary-I has become quite self-sufficient in my absence over the last couple of decades, but it remains my main project. The only project that matters at this point, at least. And soon—I consult the instruments—in just a few more hours, it shall be complete.

"Not much pleasure up there, huh?" Byrnes says. "Ever since they shut down The Space Park, it's been a drag. I used to take my youngest, but then he outgrew it anyway, so . . ." Byrnes yawns and digs into his lunch. "Mars is all the rage, yeah?"

"It's been developing rapidly, yes," I reply, watching him eat, noticing his movements slow down, his hands get heavy.

Before the tray can slip off his lap, I take it and the juice box as Byrnes's body goes limp in the seat. There is still time, so I finish his food and put the tray aside, and then I strap the captain into his seat and provide him with an oxygen mask.

In the back, I produce my luggage and take out an advanced flight suit, thin and versatile, designed to withstand immense heat and pressure. Two slim packs on the back provide oxygen and regulate temperature. I suit up but don't put the helmet on yet—one last task on my to-do list.

I produce a rollable notebook and make the final entry. Laced with regret, loss, and agony, this journey has taken decades, centuries of my life. Sacrifice has become a necessary evil and then a mundane exercise done with the same ease as making a cup of tea. Has there been love along the way? I like to think so, though the notion has become too nebulous and ephemeral to leave a lasting impression. There have been moments of serenity, stretches of time, at times decades long, where I let life take its course. Honest work, family barbecues, long walks, and camping trips. Time not wasted, but spent in waiting, in hiding. And now, mere hours away from the last movement in the never-ending symphony of time, my heartbeat is steady and my breathing is calm.

I finish the note and upload this final entry to Project Magpie, and then I break the device in two. There's nothing left to say.

In the copilot seat, I watch the moon grow larger, the dark spots of its mares clearly outlined, its halo shimmering. It looks much the same as when I first saw it up close ninety years ago—cold, uninviting, and perfect. I can almost make out the arrangements of dots, modest and almost insignificant, were it not for the secrets contained within. Soon, we near Peary-I, and the display in front of me tells me we have an hour before our scheduled descent. The crater is in sight, and the domes glisten in the sun like so many marbles neatly arranged in a circle. I take manual control of the craft.

The comms crackle, and a crystal-clear voice says, "Narwhal-3, this is Control, come in."

I tap the screen. "Narwhal-3 speaking."

"We have you on manual control, how are you doing?"

"Everything is fine here, Control," I say as I pilot the ship with as little deviation from course as I can. It's no easy task, and the shuttle yaws immediately, hundreds of kilometers off course. "Nothing to worry about, Control, just flexing the muscles. Still arriving on time."

There is a short pause and then a snicker. "I hear that, Narwhal-3. We'll keep an eye on you just the same though."

"Copy that," I reply, and I end the communication.

CHAPTER 12

They had spent the last three days following Sheriff Greene's advice. After visiting the garden office, Bloom had taken them to work. James left Tom at the engineering dome with a kiss and a promise to tell him everything that night. Work had flown by in a blink.

"It was a distraction, Tommy," he'd said, chopping cauliflower in their kitchen. "A calculated risk, if you will. I didn't really try to break into the military base, okay?"

Tom had nodded.

"I needed Greene not to worry about us as much, so we can observe and prepare."

"Are you sure about this?"

"Which part? Going after Robertson? Yes." He'd wiped his hands and joined Tom on the sofa, putting an arm around him. He'd stared at the floor for a long moment, gathering his thoughts, and Tom brushed his hair behind his ear.

"Talk to me."

James had sighed in a way Tom had seen him do so many times before. "He killed my father, Tom. I can't let this go. I need to face him. I need to talk to him, ask him . . ." James had shaken his head, his shoulders trembling in what could've been a shrug. "I need this to be over. And I need you to be with me, Tommy."

Tom hadn't replied then, and instead they'd sat in silence for a few minutes, embracing one another as their dinner boiled and steamed in the kitchen.

"I need time to think," Tom had said.

"You have a few days," James had replied.

The next day, they'd gone to work, and Tom resumed training with Sang and some others, getting through the basics of VR blueprint manipulation, getting familiar with the premises and the project, and yet every hour of that and the next two days, all he could think was—*am I going to do this?*

James had been waiting for his answer, and the pressure was almost too much to handle. Approaching the android alone would certainly get them kicked off the moon and make them both unemployable. Not to mention the media storm they'd arrive to back on Earth, and then it'd be back to life in the cold Santa Barbara mansion surrounded by cops with Tom's mom always hovering and getting drunk by the fireplace. And if James took it further? They'd both go to jail, and not the funny moon kind from James's impression of Greene.

After these thoughts corroded his mind for hours, he'd always come back to the day Rene Robertson bludgeoned James's father to death. The police sirens, the smell of copper in the hot dry air, but most of all, James, alone and shaking in his arms.

"I'll do it," Tom had said on the third day, "but you have to make a promise."

They'd been walking the Peary Square at lunch, drinking beer out of bamboo tumblers in the artificial sun. Something like a date.

"Anything," James had said.

"You will just talk. Ask your questions and leave the android be."

James had taken a swig of his beer, looking into Tom's eyes, and a cold thought had manifested: *If he says no, then this is over.*

But James hadn't said no. Instead, he'd put his arms around Tom, resting his chin on his shoulder. Tom smelled his hair, soft and silky. James said, "I love you, yeah? I promise. I just want to talk to him. That's all."

"Yeah," Tom had replied, the butterflies in his stomach putting a smile on his face. He'd bit his lip. "What do you need me to do?" Tom had hugged him back, and they'd tossed their tumblers and walked the square some more, and James told him the plan.

The next morning, on their day off, Tom woke up earlier than usual, dressed for the day, and went downstairs to make breakfast, even though he himself wouldn't be able to eat, not with all the jitters. James came down just as Tom set a coffee and a plate of French toast on the table—his favorite. "Good morning, J."

"Hey," James said, and he brushed back his hair, fixing it with the silver band. "Sleep well?"

Tom hovered over the kitchen island with a glass of water. "Barely at all. Tell me again what the plan is."

"The miners, Robertson included, will be brought over from the military facility to hang out at the square, right? Fucked if I know why robots need to go shopping, but that's the intel I got from Adelia's guy on the base." Tom frowned at that last bit but let it slide. James smelled the coffee with his eyes closed, took a sip, and continued, "They'll drive out of three o'clock sometime in the next couple hours and take a tour of sorts, going counterclockwise."

Tom closed his eyes, visualizing a military bus circling the square.

"I'm going out in twenty," James said as he took off his wristband, "to stake out the area. I'll need you to call the Sheriff and ask him to come over to get them as far away from the base as possible. Maybe you woke up and I wasn't there? Anyway, I'll take a ride on that transport and have a chat with the clunker."

Tom took a breath and then a drink. "Just a chat?"

"Just a chat. Ten minutes, maybe fifteen, depending on how many stops the bus makes."

They finished their breakfast and stepped out into the little backyard, basking in the sun. Tom's hands shook, and he flexed them, and then James said, "You'll do great, Tommy."

"I think so. I just hope it doesn't end badly." He let out a nervous laugh. "I'm trembling, so stupid."

"It's normal," James said, putting his hands on Tom's shoulders. "Take a breath. We're not doing anything illegal, per se, just messing about. After today, we'll get back to normal. Go to work and all, and maybe even to Italy someday."

Tom put his hands on James's waist. "That'd be one too many promises coming from you."

They kissed, and then James said he had to get dressed, so they went upstairs, hand in hand, aiming to put that excitement to good use.

Fifteen minutes later, Tom watched James throw on his white-and-green jumpsuit and shoes and tie his hair with a scrunchy.

"You better get out of bed too, you know," James said with a wink.

"I'm right behind you."

As soon as James went downstairs, Tom jumped out of bed and dressed, tucking his present into a hip pack. If everything went well, which he trusted it would, they could meet at The Needle later and finally celebrate the move. Go back to their new life—

His bracelet beeped then, and when he raised his hand, it projected a small hologram of an exclamation point blinking red. A recorded message advised citizens to remain where they were. *Not good.*

Downstairs, James was still in the hallway, looking through the peephole. Tom froze on the stairs, and James turned to him with a blank expression as he opened the door.

"James Mason," Sheriff Greene said. "May we come in?"

James stepped aside, and the Sheriff stepped through, followed by Deputy Bloom. Tom joined them in the kitchen.

"What's this about, Sheriff?" James said. "We were just about to go . . . shopping."

Tom swallowed. How could they know? *Did* they know? "Coffee?" he said in his most confident voice.

"Thank you, Mr. Brown-Allen. The issue is this. Rene Robertson is missing. He was last seen on his way into Peary-I proper, but . . ." The Sheriff pursed his lips and blinked. "Any idea where he might have gone?"

Deputy Bloom took a step toward the stairs, and Tom watched him closely.

Sheriff Greene said, "If you'd like to share anything, either of you, now would be the time."

James glanced at Tom, who only shrugged, vaguely aware of his knees trembling. Gone was Greene's kind-garden-gnome attitude. That seemed to be it for their grand plan. James drummed his fingers on the kitchen island.

"There could be something . . ." he said. "But I'd need to talk to whoever you've talked to first. You know, make sure we're all on the same page about this."

No, no, no . . .

The Sheriff said, "You want to come into the station?"

"I'd like to clear things up. For the record, I have nothing to do with the clunker's disappearance, but as far as I'm concerned, he can stay lost."

Tom managed, "I'd like to come along."

"By all means," the Sheriff replied, inviting everyone to leave.

On the way to Bloom's car, when they had a moment to themselves, just the two of them, Tom said, "What are we doing?"

"Improvising," James whispered. "Trust me."

They filed into the back of the car, James taking the seat behind the driver. Their fingers laced, they sat quietly as the vehicle buzzed down the residential tunnels toward Peary Square. Somehow, in that moment, Tom felt calmer than he had since their arrival. The plan was essentially over, and whatever James was up to at the Security Station would likely amount to little but killing time and covering their asses. Safer there, at any rate, next to the Sheriff and away from trouble.

Rene Robertson was a miner, venturing out beyond the crater to the North Pole and the dark side of the moon. Who knew where he could've gone or what kind of business these sentient robots were involved in at the military installation? All that mattered was that James was by his side.

As they neared the square, all three bracelets and the central console in the vehicle went off, all blinking red with seemingly new vigor.

"Ten-thirteen, boss," Bloom said.

"Just what we needed," the Sheriff grumbled as they entered the roundabout. "Meteorites. Don't worry, that's why we have the lasers."

They all stared up through the clear glass roof of the car, ready to watch the fireworks.

"Not a meteorite, sir," Bloom said, hitting the brakes. Their vehicle slid across the roundabout and hit the curb, rattling its passengers about, and came to rest on the sidewalk.

"What the fuck?" James said, and Tom felt his grip tighten.

Above the Peary Square dome, a space shuttle grew larger by the second, its white hull glistening in the sun. Perhaps this was a glitch in the projection on the dome's ceiling or some cruel prank . . . perhaps James had orchestrated this as another properly insane diversion. There had to be some mistake, at any rate. Why would a shuttle be flying toward them?

"Seat belts, everyone," barked Greene.

Tom found himself mentally detached from the situation as if he were watching a film or a particularly vivid dream. He looked around to see James with his eyes wide and mouth agape, hastily fastening the four-point belt.

He glanced back through the roof, and there it was, only for a split second. Crisp and clear and outlined against the black sky was the nose of a cargo shuttle, white and black and shiny. A moment later, all air and sound was sucked out of the dome, and immense heat—

CHAPTER 13

——

The ground was warm beneath his cheek, but his body trembled, each movement sending jolts of pain throughout. James's head throbbed at the temple. As he slowly regained bodily control, he felt his fists still clutching the straps of the seat belt on his chest, which was pressing him tightly into the seat. He gasped for air, inhaled dust, and coughed it up onto the tarmac, spitting a gray mass. He felt for the belt's release lever. When he found it, he rolled out of the seat onto his chest, smearing the ground with blood.

The seat itself had been ripped out of the vehicle and lay broken in the middle of the road. Gasping, James got to all fours and then slowly up, holding on to the seat for balance, his vision swimming. He brushed back his hair, smearing his hand with dirt and blood, and then wiping it on his jumpsuit.

Through clouds of smoke and dust, he first saw deep skid marks, as if someone had plowed the tarmac, stretching across the square. James looked himself over, checking for injuries and finding none, and then stumbled . . . somewhere, anywhere, looking for . . . *Tom.*

He remembered the car stopping just outside the residential tunnel at nine o'clock, but now, looking around at the desolate square, it was impossible to tell which direction that had been. Glass crunched under his feet, and he felt it but couldn't quite hear the sound. He saw wheels and crumpled panels among the concrete and steel debris strewn around the square. A broken umbrella with the Luna Cafe logo lazily twirled across, as if also surveying the damage. The cafe itself was nowhere to be found.

And that's when suppressed moans reached him through the smoke, weak and inhuman. James took a few more steps toward what he realized was the wreck of the cafe, its frame collapsed, metal panels hanging loosely. Had it exploded? Seemed that way. But then he saw those same plow marks and pools and splatters of blood mixed with dust and debris where tables had been. In the distance, obscured by the smoke, someone was crawling, dragging their useless, bloodied legs behind. Sound seeped into James's ears more clearly now: someone cried, more people shouted orders, and alarms trilled in the distance. The dome must have sealed, and the air-filtering systems buzzed, working overtime trying to clear the dust.

"Tom!" James yelled in a raspy voice. "Where are you, babe?"

Still struggling to tell which direction he was going, he stumbled on along the scorch marks, stepping over bits and pieces of . . . yes, it had been a shuttle. It really had crashed into Peary-I. James's breath quickened as he sucked in somewhat less polluted air.

"Tommy!"

He didn't immediately recognize Bloom's car, mainly because of how little of it was left. Its metal frame, resting on the sidewalk across the road, had been smashed and crumpled as if a truck had hit it at a hundred miles per hour. All glass had shattered, and wheels and panels had come off and scattered.

"Tom!"

James ran, limping, ignoring for the time being the crashed cargo shuttle wedged in the twelve o'clock tunnel, still burning.

"Fuck . . ."

In the passenger seat, Sheriff Greene's decapitated body was still strapped to the seat, and next to him, the steering wheel had flattened Deputy Bloom's chest. The rear of the cabin had remained more intact—minus James's seat—and Tom was strapped into his still, but . . .

As James neared the wreck, he saw the lower half of Tom's jumpsuit soaked in blood, painting it maroon red. Tommy himself was pale, his head on his chest, arms limp at his sides.

James fell to his knees at Tom's side, fiddling with the seat belt. The mechanism had locked, Tom's full weight tightening the belt. The lever wouldn't give. "Come on, Tommy, we gotta go now . . ." He tried to check for Tom's breathing, but couldn't focus or hear anything, and so he tugged on the belt, too afraid to move Tom's body.

"Let me help," someone said behind him.

James snapped around and froze at the sight of Rene Robertson. His lips trembling, James said, "What the fuck did you do?"

"I assure you, I had nothing to do with this, James. Here. He doesn't have much time."

The android reached into the mangled vehicle and wrapped a fist around the seat belt lock, crushing it to bits. As soon as that pressure was gone, Tom sucked in a short, arrested breath and coughed up blood.

"Tommy, I'm here." James held his face in both hands. "Look at me, I'm here."

Tom did, but his eyes rolled in his head and didn't focus. "Pack . . ."

James glanced down and said, "It's there, but we need to go." He snapped his head to the android. "Tell him, you fucker!"

Rene Robertson remained standing, waiting. "There's nothing I can do."

Tom whispered, "The pack . . . for you . . ." His right hand, poorly coordinated, felt for his hip pack, opened it, and rummaged around. Tom brought up a small pouch, soaked in blood. "Take . . ."

James did, not sure what to do with it just then, so he simply held it tight. Wiping his face, mixing blood with tears, James embraced Tom. Seconds stretched as they sat like this, and James got lost in the moment so much that he didn't even notice when Tom stopped breathing.

"We do need to go, James," the clunker said, and more than ever, James wanted to kill him.

"I'm not leaving."

"You have to, or we're both dead."

The android put a hand on his shoulder, and James shot up to his feet, pivoting to strike. Rene caught his wrist, locking it in a steel grip, and lifted James slightly, only letting him keep his toes on the ground. He turned him around. "Look."

A hundred feet away, the wreck of the cargo shuttle smoked, its emergency light flickering, and then a hatch hissed and fell off, landing on the tarmac with a dull clang. Rene lowered James, and they watched as a dark figure emerged from the opening, grabbing the edges and observing the square. A survivor, dressed in a reflective suit of some kind, but not standard issue. The figure hopped down and landed on both feet, taking a step to catch their balance.

"Maybe they can help us," James whimpered.

"No," Rene replied. "We should get going."

Just then, the figure snapped its head, and even through the reflective helmet, James felt its gaze on him. He turned to Tom and gave him one last, short embrace, kissing his cold cheek, shivering as he did so. When he got up, Rene was already walking away toward a military-issue vehicle. The figure from the shuttle started toward them, and James caught up to the android, hopping into the vehicle next to him. As soon as he shut the door, they sped off.

The android dodged debris without a mistake, his synthetic mind calculating trajectories before James could even see the obstacles, no matter the smoke and dust in the air.

"Where are we going?"

"The military installation."

"Why?"

"That's the only safe place for you."

James studied Rene, whose face betrayed no emotion. Too many questions fought for attention in his brain, and all he could do was stare. James glanced at his hands. His right one still clutched the blood-soaked pouch. He'd been vaguely aware of it this whole time, its odd shape and wet, cold texture, and now he carefully unwrapped it. Tears blurred his vision, and he wiped them and stared at a greeting card—damp with blood but still readable—a cartoon moon with hearts for eyes that said, "Over the moon for you!"

He wanted to fold it, to save it, but only managed to tear it apart. He let go of the dissolving piece of paper and was left with a small box he couldn't bring himself to open. Instead, he tucked it into his hip pack and wiped his hands on the seat.

"I'm sorry about Thomas," Rene said.

"Who was it, in the shuttle?"

"Haywood Williams."

"Dr. Williams? The scientist? The one who created you?"

The robot nodded with something like disinterest. "Among other things, yes."

They turned into the three o'clock tunnel and whizzed through the gates that stood open, red lights blinking nonstop. Nobody tried to block their way.

"Why did he do it?"

"Haywood believes this was meant to be. Fate, as it were, though he would read you a lecture on physics to support his point of view."

The words made a little sense to James. He'd only met the man once, out of the blue, when the scientist offered them jobs, and even in that short exchange, James had glimpsed uncanny resolve and confidence in the man. Dr. Haywood Williams, a brilliant scientist and formerly a pioneer in robotics and space exploration, turned out to be nothing but a maniac.

"He brought us here on purpose," James said to no one in particular.

"Indeed."

The tunnel dipped and took them below ground, and what little sunlight had been illuminating it gave way to exclusively artificial lighting.

"I don't understand."

"You will."

The facility's utilitarian interior design continued here, with stark angles and dark walls, and as they passed by smaller tunnels, James caught glimpses of laboratories and offices.

"What did you do here?" he asked, surprising even himself. "What did you mine?"

Rene turned and gave him a sly smile. "So much I'd like to tell you, James, but I'm afraid we don't have the luxury of time. We're here."

He took a turn into a narrow tunnel, and they stopped in front of a set of bright yellow doors adorned with various warning graphics, not big enough for the vehicle to pass. Rene scanned his wrist, and the doors hissed open, letting them through. They walked a narrow hallway, and the robot scanned his wrist twice more. A system of hallways and ladders took them down two stories until they emerged into a dimly lit space big enough to house a shuttle but lacking any doors bigger than a human.

I could just kill him here, James thought, absurdly, and smirked. "Where are we?"

Rene walked to a computer terminal and typed, and a moment later, a dark shape materialized at the center of the hangar. The large craft shaped like a saucer was seemingly fixed in space a few feet above the ground—not hovering, but just . . . sitting there. Its surface reflected the dim lights, but only enough to give it a sense of shape. The craft hissed then, and a ramp lowered to the floor. James stood there for a long moment, taking in the sight.

"This is your way out, James," Rene said, joining him. "You need to get in before Haywood gets here, which is . . . within the next two minutes."

"I can't."

"But you do."

James glanced at the android, his features up close soft and somehow reassuring. Whatever rage had brewed inside him was suddenly gone, overshadowed by this new revelation.

Had he been planning to kill Rene? He'd certainly fantasized about it on a daily basis, even though deep down, he knew it would be physically impossible. But now, the synthetic man seemed to be the only other person in the world, and James was secretly glad to have him in his corner.

As if reading his mind, Rene said, "Before you go, I believe you have a question for me, James."

James swallowed, his eyes watering, his heart racing. Suddenly, he wasn't ready. "Why'd you kill my dad?" he blurted out.

Rene held his gaze, his brows slightly furrowed, and said, "You asked me to."

CHAPTER 14

———

Stepping onto the smooth rubberized trap, James hesitated. He inhaled the air, ionized and new in a way that any recently manufactured machine smelled—of electronics, polished steel, and fresh leather. Up the ramp, dim lights illuminated the interior, and not much else was visible yet. Was this alien tech? Everything James knew of interstellar research—outside of wacky conspiracy theories—told him intelligent life beyond Earth and the colonies had not yet been discovered. And whatever UFOs had been sighted had never been confirmed to be . . . well, anything other than that.

He took another step. The craft didn't sway or creak or show any other sign of having felt the added weight.

In an anxious trance, James ascended the ramp of the flying saucer and found himself in a pristine cockpit—a windowless round deck with two seats in the middle with integrated instrument panels. As soon as he stood on the floor, the ramp behind him hissed and closed, sealing the craft. Fresh air pumped into the cabin with a barely audible buzz. Once it stopped, the silence deafened James, and the cold, sterile space reminded him of an interrogation room or a morgue. He half-expected aliens to step in and strap him into the chair or the room to fill with some kind of toxic gas.

Neither happened, and the long moment was finally broken by a voice seemingly in his own head. "Please take a seat."

"Rene?"

"No, sir," the voice replied, its tone low and measured. "This is the ship speaking. But my timbre does imitate your friend Rene Robertson."

"He's not my fucking friend, so you better drop the timbre."

"Noted." In a more feminine voice, it said, "Please sit, as I am initiating the jump sequence. *Now.*"

Reluctantly, James did, limping over and climbing into one of the seats. The interface remained a blank panel of glistening brushed aluminum, and the faux leather was cool and stiff. James buckled the belt across his chest, wincing from pain.

"What's happening outside?" he said, and immediately the dome of the saucer turned clear, showcasing the interior of the hangar around them.

Below, near the computer terminal, Rene stood facing the entrance they'd come from. The mangled figure of Dr. Haywood Williams entered through that same door, swaying as he steadied himself on a railing. With his free hand, he pulled off the helmet, revealing ruffled white hair and a bloodied face. He stared at Rene and then beyond, his eyes searching for the cloaked flying saucer. The android put a hand on his chest, but Williams brushed it off. They were arguing now.

"What the fuck is taking so long?" James yelled, slamming a fist on the panel in front of him.

"Refrain from damaging the equipment. I am confirming the positions of celestial bodies. The solar system constantly accelerates through the universe and—" In a more urgent tone, the computer said, "Brace yourself."

James sucked in a breath and held it, clenching the seat belt. The next moment, air was forced out of his lungs as the surrounding screens went black, radiating a weak white light. James struggled to breathe, and when a motor buzzed somewhere again, pumping in more cold air, he panted.

"What happened?" he said, turning his head in search of an answer. "Where are they?"

Although the force of gravity had not changed, James realized the craft was slowly tilting left—no, fully rotating. From the corner of his eye, he saw the tiny bluish-white speck of the Earth. And then the moon filled the view, coming in from the left and overtaking the transparent dome above James's head. His mind spun from the bizarre notion of hanging upside down above the moon, strapped in a pilot's seat and pressed to the floor as if bolted to a small platform floating in space.

"First test jump performed successfully," the computer said. "Your vital signs are within acceptable parameters, although you might be experiencing dizziness."

"Thanks," James replied, swallowing as he stared up at the moon. "Did we just . . . fucking teleport?"

After a pause, the computer replied, "Yes and no." Its female voice was far less grating to James's ear than Rene's, though there was still some condescension in it.

"But we are in space above the moon, right? This isn't a projection."

"It is not. You are seeing what is directly above us right now. We are moving toward the Peary-I research facility on the moon of Earth."

"We need to get down there," James said. "People down there are dying. We need to call someone!"

The computer didn't reply, but the craft did seem to accelerate. James searched the glowing globe and found the base. How fast were they going now? He didn't want to ask the AI, but it had to be faster than what he'd experienced in the shuttle *Hypervelocity*. Moments later, he could tell the domes of the base apart and the Spaceport on the right. It looked . . . normal. The central dome must've been sealed perfectly, but how could that be?

"Get me down there!"

"I'm afraid this is as far as my protocols will let us travel, Mr. Mason."

"Fuck your protocols," James yelled, and he unstrapped the harness and jumped out of the seat.

Despite all the bells going off in his lizard brain about being on the edge of the abyss, he leaped to the invisible wall of the flying saucer, fingers sprawled against its cold invisible metal. "I need to get down there . . . Wait. The dome is not damaged *at all*."

"Not yet," the computer replied. "We did teleport, as you rightly noted, but we didn't just travel through space. We also traveled twenty-three minutes into the past."

James stared at Peary-I. "You mean before . . . That means . . . Get me down there!"

But the craft was fixed in place, unmoving, as if tethered to the station by an impossibly long invisible thread.

"I said let's go!" James yelled, banging on the walls, each blow landing with a dull thud.

Something darted through space then, a white speck aimed at the station from the direction of the Spaceport, and it showed no sign of slowing down. Subconsciously, on some deep level of understanding, James knew what it was even before his brain processed the thought. Watching the scene unfold from this aerial view, he was oddly fascinated by the absurdity of it—a space shuttle steadily moving toward the moon station and entering the dome's surface with a smooth, inaudible puff of debris that traveled far and wide like smoke.

"This can't be it," James whispered. "This can't be it."

"Get in the seat, please," the computer said.

Down on Peary, the dome had sealed, and the debris had dissipated, now only specks of dust getting lost on the gray surface. The shuttles at the spaceport became stationary, and all movement seized. He watched the pale still life of the moon's surface, the shimmering globes in the Peary Crater like so many spoiled fruits in a bowl.

Tom was dead.

James recoiled and stumbled a few steps back until he hit the cold instrument panel.

"We need to go," the computer said, and James turned around, crawling around the terminal and into the seat.

As he stared at nothing, his hands worked to strap the harness, and then they dropped limp in his lap. Tom was dead. Again. Still.

"The second test jump takes us to an enclosed space. Initiating sequence, calculating . . ." the computer murmured, its voice distant and unimportant.

The next moment, the moon disappeared, and James gasped for air as the deck filled with subdued light and fresh oxygen. This time, the walls remained blank. He sat in silence, not really waiting for anything, hoping the moment would stretch out, and that maybe he could spend some time in the quiet safety of the craft. But something was different. The pressure on his body had shifted ever so slightly to being pleasantly, unobtrusively familiar—no longer artificial. It didn't pull him down so much as just let him be.

"Are we back?" James said.

"Back? If you mean my Peary-I hangar, then, no, we're not back. But considering you hail from Earth, James, then we *are* back in that sense."

James snapped his head up. "We're on Earth? Now? I mean, when even is *now*?"

"Five days before your first test jump, James. My data shows this is the day you and Thomas Brown-Allen arrived at Cape Canaveral Spaceport to—"

"We're in Florida right now?" James cried, clicking the harness open. "On the day of our flight to the moon?" He lunged out of the chair and spun around on the deck, identifying the slit in the wall where the ramp had to be. "Let me the fuck out."

"I advise against venturing out before you have received your orientation, James."

"Open the hatch."

Without further protest, the ramp cracked open and lowered gently with a hiss, and James jumped down to the cement floor before it touched down. He found himself in another hangar, this one twice as big as the one they'd left on the moon—if the AI had told the truth—its walls lined with sound-dampening foam and perforated metal. The space was empty of people or any kind of electronics, and as James looked around, he searched for anything resembling a door. Behind him, the flying saucer, decloaked, was fixed once again in place a few feet above the ground. Silent, unmoving.

James walked the perimeter, feeling out the wall, pressing down on the panels until one seemed to give, and then he grabbed it, pushing his fingers deep into the holes and pulling as hard as he could, pressing at the wall with a foot for extra leverage. The door gave and let James into a long, dark corridor of cement floor and walls with thin LED strips on the ceiling that filled it with white light. He hesitated for a moment, and then the heavy door softly closed, pushing him forward. Whatever this place was, he had to get out.

The corridor ended at a set of service elevator doors and a locked door that presumably led to the stairs. James smashed the button. The doors opened quickly, and inside, he pressed a button with a star next to it. The cabin shot up, and James had to bend his knees slightly to resist the pull, then it came to a stop just as swiftly. He stepped out.

Another corridor brought him to a door marked *Gates*. He peeked out, and his jaw hung open. It was as if he'd stepped straight into a memory of the bright fall day they'd left the planet. The Spaceport terminal buzzed and moved at its own pace, too slowly for James's erratic, adrenaline-driven brain. People smiled, laughed, and walked about without a care in the world, apart from an occasional runner late for their flight or a tired parent sprawled in a chair in the waiting area.

He stumbled out and crossed the floor, searching every face in the crowd, trying to think back to the day that already seemed months in the past. Except it wasn't. It had become today, *now*. What little logical thinking he could muster told James the past version of himself was drinking at one bar or another, some dark lounge hidden away behind heavy curtains. Which meant the past version of Tom was perusing the shops, looking for . . . *the postcard*.

Where would he go?

The card would've taken Tom some time to pick. So, a bookstore.

He pushed through the crowds, vaguely aware of people recoiling from him, shooting him frowns, and someone yelling, "Hey!"

No time for that. His bloodstained jumpsuit left dusty marks on passersby, and James didn't care. The bookstore. James jumped up, letting out a low, creaky noise, as his lame leg sent a bolt of pain to his groin.

But there was Tom, alive and glowing, as he danced along bookshelves, lightly touching things and stopping himself before he got too carried away on his way to the magazine stand. James wanted to call out, but the yell got stuck in his throat, and he instead focused on the perfect image of Tom, alive still and careless and beautiful.

For a split second, he saw Tom look up, squinting, a perfect portrait of his beloved—and then a hand shoved James in the chest, and he went down on his ass. Towering above him, a young woman with an angry expression on her face was pointing a gun at his.

"Stay down, Mr. Mason," she said through clenched teeth, and then addressed the people around them, "Spaceport security! Give us some space."

As she repelled the crowd with a stare, James noted the black uniform she wore. A light gunmetal exoskeleton supported her full body and wrapped her arms and legs. It was no security gear he'd ever seen.

She lowered the weapon to keep it out of sight. "Get up, slowly."

James did, grunting from pain and then dusting off his hands. "I need to go."

"Don't you ever," she said. "Move it."

She was a head shorter and looked a year or two younger than him with a fresh buzz cut and a scar on her left cheek.

He stared her down, and she held his gaze without blinking, her jaw clenched.

"I need to—"

"No, you don't. You're going back." And she raised the weapon slightly to make the point.

James walked. Maybe he could break away, get lost in the crowd, and circle back to the bookstore? All he needed was ten seconds with Tom to tell him what was going to happen, to see him up close once again, to touch his hand. A hot flash struck him with a feeling of helplessness, of being led to slaughter. But he walked.

When they entered the *Staff Only* corridor, he said, "I'm James, by the way. But I guess you know that already."

"I do. Keep moving," she replied, and she poked him with the barrel of the gun.

"What's your name?"

"Don't try to establish rapport with me, Mr. Mason. That's a sure way of getting shot."

They entered the elevator, her gun still pressing firmly into the small of his back, and James held his hands up. "You're going to kill me?"

She smirked. "I'd love to, but those aren't my orders. I'm to get you on the flying saucer."

The elevator dinged, and she nudged him forward.

"And who gave the orders?" he said. "Aliens?"

"You're funny, Mr. Mason."

As they walked down the brightly illuminated corridor, James was hoping for someone to pop out and confront them. Maybe whoever ran the place wouldn't be too pleased about the whole situation. Unless, of course, the woman worked for whoever had organized his little trip. Haywood Williams? It seemed likely.

They reached the heavy door of the hangar and stopped. "Open it."

"It's pretty heavy."

"Didn't stop you the first time, did it?"

"Right. I'll try to push it open, but I can't promise you anything," he said, planting his feet and leaning against the cold metal.

The door gave easily enough and cracked open, but he'd exaggerated its weight, and as soon as he had enough space, James fell through the opening. Once inside, he caught his balance and shifted it back, pressing the door closed.

"Mason!" the woman yelled, and she managed to pop her gun-wielding hand through the crack. "Open it!"

"I don't think so!" James panted, but his shoes had enough grip on the cement floor to keep the pressure on.

Her exoskeleton-bound arm clanged between the door and the frame, metal joints buzzing as she tried to bend her wrist to get a good shot. She didn't take it, probably because she might've actually hit him, and James was grateful. Seconds later, the mechanisms malfunctioned, letting out a sharp pop and a sad whiz, and the gun fell out of the woman's hand.

Without thinking, James snatched it, leaping toward the sealed saucer, and then he snapped around, aiming the gun at the door. Behind him, the ramp hissed and lowered. Ahead, the woman entered, flexing one hand. In the other, she held an identical handgun, pointed at him. James's hand trembled. Hers didn't.

"Step up that ramp, James," she said in an even tone. "There's no getting out of here for you."

"I have a gun too, you know."

She smirked. "Boy, do I. Hold on tight to it. You'll need it."

James considered shooting her. At this range, he could probably hit her, too, if she didn't shoot back. He'd never held a gun before, had never aimed one at anyone. James was more of a talker, anyway. "I need to find Tom Brown-Allen."

"I know, and you will. Find him, I mean." She jerked her gun at the flying saucer. "There. That's your ticket, Mr. Mason. Just walk up that ramp. Simple as that."

Reluctantly, James lowered the gun with a deep sigh. "Is it?"

"No," the woman replied, still holding her gun steady in the air.

James backed away one step, then two, watching her. Before he disappeared inside, he said, "What's your name?"

"Carmen."

CHAPTER 15

My daughter may be dying out in the desert as I drive west across the state line and back to California. Mountain ranges, black as a wall beyond the desert, are outlined against the dark sky splattered with stars. My destination—Los Albertos Forest Trail Inn, a few hours away from Silver Peak.

It is a remote getaway, and the last twenty minutes of the ride I spend navigating a narrow forest trail, the wheels of the car I borrowed from the men in black tearing through the ruts, dry weeds scraping the bottom. I arrive at the cabin shortly before dawn and bring the car to a halt at the porch.

The small wooden building tucked away in a dark corner of the forest seems uninhabited—still and quiet, it almost manages to fit in with the dense trees surrounding it, its roof covered with a thin layer of moss, vines climbing up the support beams of the canopy. The engine powers down and lights subside, and I step out to take the few creaky steps up to the porch. My knocking breaks the silence momentarily, and I am left to stand there, hoping I'm at the right place. I spend a few minutes leaning on the wooden railing and observe the dark and chilly forest beyond, wondering if anything is looking back at me, imagining myself in its place—hidden by the dark, free to roam these woods as part of it . . .

A dim yellow light comes to life inside and illuminates the porch. Muffled steps on the other side of the door, and then, without being unlocked, it opens with a characteristic creak. I turn around.

"Hello, Haywood."

"Good morning." I reach out for a handshake, but the host does not return it.

"What brings you here?" Rene stands blocking the doorway, though his face betrays no emotion. He wears a white T-shirt and pants to match, his hair ruffled.

"Did I wake you?"

"I rested, yes."

"May I come in?" After a moment, he steps aside, and I walk into the cabin, fittingly ascetic—a thin mattress on a simple bed frame in a corner, a nightstand, and a cupboard. On the mantle of the crackling fireplace, incense sticks produce thin trails of gray smoke and fill the room with a smell of lavender, and the worn leather armchair to its left looks warm and inviting.

"Please, sit, Haywood," Rene says, shutting the door, and I smile up at him. "What is this about?"

"You've been away a long time, my friend," I say.

"Twenty years, yes. I needed time to think."

"Well, I'm afraid the time is up."

Rene paces the room—no more than three steps back and forth—and then he stops at the windows to watch the sunrise. With every second, more golden light fills the room, outlining his form on the front door. I wait.

"Everything I know of this world," Rene says, "everything I have observed over the last century and have come to believe, it all screams at me to kick you out. I should let you be on your way, wherever that takes you. I don't want to know." He won't turn to look at me as he squints at the sun. "Haven't you done enough violence, Haywood?"

He knows all my answers, of course, as I know all his questions, so I don't immediately speak. When I do, it's a genuine attempt to comfort him. "I admire and respect your philosophy, Rene, and I am proud of the way you have turned out."

"There he goes," Rene sighs at the window, but he does turn to listen.

"It has never been my intention to involve you or compromise your beliefs, nor does it bring me any pleasure to interrupt your retreat. I don't want to—"

"You want me to kill a man," Rene says, and for the first time maybe ever, I hear contempt in his voice. He steps away from the window, and only a low coffee table separates us. "You come here and drag in with you your sorry theories and prophecies built on death, Haywood. And you have the audacity to ask that I fulfill your vision?"

The eye contact is only broken when I glance away. Rene is not wrong, little as he may see of the big picture.

"Not at all," I say, and I give him a moment to sit down on his bed. "The last thing I want is to see my friend kill another man. Twenty years ago, when James asked you to kill Frankie Mason, you walked away, even though you knew—"

"I needed time to meditate on it."

"And I supported your decision."

"Reluctantly."

"Even so. You are aware of my beliefs as much as I am of yours, and it took a toll to go against my truth"—Rene rolls his eyes, but I continue—"but today I'm not here for me. I've been away from the Providence Foundation for a while now, and in my absence, Frankie Mason—"

Rene raises a hand. "I don't believe you, Haywood. You are incapable of staying away, of letting someone else control the narrative. This ham-fisted manipulation does not become you."

I nod. Years of isolation have neither stripped Rene of his sharp mind nor affected his memory. Of all of my companions, he's known me the longest. Except, of course, James. "I apologize, old friend. I shouldn't have tried to swindle you like that. In truth, I have been involved in the events of the past few decades no less than I had before, and I've been watching Frankie Mason closely. James told you the truth about him. Frankie Mason is a liar and a murderer."

"You must be good friends." His hands grip the edge of the bed, creasing the pristinely folded blanket.

"You know there's only one reason I could be here now, today, at this hour." I stand up and wait for his response, but it doesn't come. "We are both in service of the vision, Rene, both destined to fulfill it. Our beliefs are immaterial, but time is of the essence. If I'm here . . ." I spread my arms and then take a step toward the door. Behind me, Rene makes no attempt to move.

"So," he says, "if we sit here for a couple more hours . . ."

"I met the Traveler earlier today, out in Nevada. This is what happens."

The android stares, and this time I hold his gaze. He says, "Is that so, Haywood?"

"You know I wouldn't be here if it weren't." I glance at my watch and add, "Come. He's meeting you for the first time in a few hours. I'll tell you more on the way."

I leave to wait for him in the idling car, watching the forest fill with light and life, birds chirping, squirrels hopping between trunks. Minutes pass, and then Rene appears in the door, wearing his signature trench coat and hat.

CHAPTER 16

———

The hatch closed, and James lingered on the deck for a long moment, the gun raised again, waiting for Carmen to tear through the metal and get him. He'd never shot anyone before, but today—whatever that had become—his finger was itchy on the trigger, looking for a target. The flying saucer hummed to life, and when nobody came in the hatch, James lowered the weapon.

"Did she tell me the truth?" he managed.

"I have no way of knowing," the computer replied. And then added, "She did seem to be convinced of her words, however. Besides, the next jump takes us further into the relative past, so we can't rule out the possibility of you meeting Thomas Brown-Allen."

James did a one-eighty and stepped up to the pilot's seat. "Start the next jump," he ordered. "And show me Carmen."

"Already on it," the computer replied. "Calculating . . ."

As he stepped away from the sealed hatch, the walls became transparent, but the woman was no longer out there. He considered going after her, after Tom, up there in the spaceport, careless and alone. How could he face him now? No, there had to be another way, a better time for it. He climbed into the pilot's seat and strapped in, hiding the gun in a storage recess under the armrest.

"What's taking so long?"

"Have I mentioned that your solar system is traveling through the universe?" the computer said with a tinge of sarcasm. "I did not come up with the laws of physics, Mr. Mason. I simply follow them."

"Fine, yeah," he said, rubbing his eyes and brushing back his hair. "Can you get on with it, though?"

"The next jump takes us back almost a year, which amounts to tens of billions of kilometers traveled, and that's not taking into account the finer movement and rotations of planets and—"

"I get it, alright? Go."

The deck went silent, and James drummed his fingers on the cold panel in front of him, his foot tapping incessantly on the platform. The machine hummed and clicked somewhere below deck, sending a barely perceptible vibration through the seat as it powered up. The temperature might've raised slightly.

"What do I call you?" James said. "Unless I'm distracting you."

"My official designation is Project Magpie."

"Magpie? Like the bird?"

"I suppose."

"Mysterious. So, Magpie, you're a time machine made to look like a flying saucer, huh?" Even as he said the words, James couldn't quite process or believe them. A part of him still expected this all to be a hoax, or an elaborate illusion designed to test his mental endurance, or maybe to simulate . . . he didn't know what. It had to be some kind of test he'd walked into in that military hangar. "Just to make sure, this is all real, yeah?"

Magpie paused, then said, "I'm afraid so."

James didn't speak again, squeezing the armrests and staying perfectly still, taking short gulps of air to catch the moment when he'd need to breathe out before the jump.

"Almost there," Magpie assured him. "These will get easier to handle. Aaand . . . now."

James exhaled and felt the saucer jitter and spin before artificial gravity fixed him in place. Moments later, they stabilized, gently leveling and gliding through the clouds. The 360-degree view of the sky messed with James's head, and he had to shut his eyes.

"Sorry about that," Magpie said. "We popped in upside down."

"Excellent. Just bring us down."

"Could've been worse. We could've—"

"I don't care. Land!" The saucer began its descent, and James opened his eyes to see the eerily familiar shoreline below, green and brown with a beige-and-white strip where the beach met the ocean. He really was there, almost a year ago, which meant . . . "What's the date?"

"May 6, 2125, the day of—"

"Fuck. I know," James said, and his hand reached down to grab the gun. "Get us down."

"May I advise a course of action?"

"No. I know what to do."

It couldn't be a mistake. The saucer brought him here, to this day, snatched him from the moon and spat him out over 'Cito. His fingers tightened around the grip of the gun, his index finger tapping the guard. The craft lowered, not falling or losing altitude but steadily moving downward, making it look as if the planet was moving toward them.

James thought he saw his house in the distance, and then hills grew around the saucer as it lowered into a canyon. "I hope you're cloaked, Magpie," he said.

"Always."

They touched down in a dusty clearing, surrounded by rocks and scraggly bushes and trees. Not hidden, exactly, but secluded enough. James hopped out of the chair, gun at his side. "Let me out."

Magpie did so, opening the hatch and letting in a tidal wave of hot, dry air that knocked James back. He tucked the gun away and walked down the ramp, stepping onto hot sand. At the edge of the clearing, he observed the flat slab of Montecito below, covered in dark green trees like moss with occasional pale red spots of tile roofs connected by gray strips of road. James walked through coarse bushes to the nearest footpath as if in a trance, the legs of his jumpsuit catching on thorns as his hands flexed, eager to feel that gun again.

The path led him to a road woven through the hills, and he stomped his feet to dust off his boots and walked along the shoulder. Down below, less than a mile, it would bring him to the narrow road ending in a cobbled driveway. No time to lose. James stepped quicker, almost jogging, trying to keep his breathing steady as his brain rehearsed everything he'd say to the android before putting a bullet through his head. Right here, on this road, before he ever got a chance to walk into his house in that fucking hat of his and that innocent fucking smile.

The sun scorched his head, and he ran out of breath, slowing down to swallow and wipe sweat off his face. "Fuck!"

A hundred feet from the turn, he drew the gun and felt its weight, inspecting it as if to make sure it was in proper working order—in truth, he had no idea how it worked. What he could do was visualize squeezing the trigger and letting out a shot. Simple enough.

Just as he was about to step off the asphalt and turn onto the narrow path, a black sedan appeared at the top of the road behind him, headed his way, and James jerked around, hiding the gun-wielding hand behind his back. The police? Was he too late? Were they there for him? The odd matte-black vehicle skidded to a stop in front of him, two wheels off the road, and James froze. His already rattled brain went into overdrive, imagining shooting at whoever emerged from the vehicle and carrying on with the mission, and it forced his hand to raise the gun.

The driver's door swung open, and out stepped, not a policeman, but Dr. Haywood Williams. James's hand trembled as he traced the man's movement with the muzzle. Williams raised his hands, circling the car in a couple strides.

"I'm here to help, James," he said. He wore some kind of military uniform with a long jacket over deep blue overalls fitted with a belt.

"Like you helped on the moon?"

Williams frowned. "That hasn't happened yet, not for me."

"And if I shoot you, it will never happen."

"You're wrong."

That's when the passenger door opened, and Rene Robertson stepped onto the dusty shoulder, one hand holding the brim of his hat. "We meet again, James."

The muzzle swung over to the android, and he stepped over. The two men James hated most now stood just a few feet apart. Williams lowered his hands, and they stood in silence for a minute, James's gun moving side to side before finally settling on Rene's chest. From this distance, barely thirty feet, he felt confident enough in hitting the clunker.

"You killed my father. I watched you bash his head in." And then he swung the gun over to Williams. "But you! You killed Tommy. Crushed him like a puppet. Why?" The gun trembled once again, and he steadied it on the man's chest.

Williams shut his eyes as if the words physically hurt him. "He was a casualty."

Before James could think anything, his finger pulled the trigger. At the same exact time, the android's arm shot up, his hand blocking Williams, exploding with yellow sparks and a trickle of black smoke. The robot cried and pulled the arm back, and then lunged forward. James shot again but missed, and the next moment the android was in front of him, slapping the gun out of his hand and shoving him back with incredible force. James stumbled but held his ground, gasping for air. His teeth clenched, he attempted to fight back, but Rene grabbed him by the collar, lifted him up, and smashed him into the dusty ground.

James rolled over, coughing and grasping at his chest, looking for the gun and not finding it. His voice creaked when he said, "Why did I ask you to do it?"

"I can't say." Rene held onto his shot-up hand, and then he hid it in his trench coat and stood there, expectantly glancing at Williams. There was new resolve in his face, as if the shooting sealed the deal.

James sat up and dusted off his hands.

Williams had recoiled from the shot and was now leaning on the vehicle, holding the gun. "You really scared me there, James. Please, get up. Give me a chance to explain."

The android touched the brim of his hat with two fingers, holding it in place against a gust of wind. James wanted to go after him, but he struggled to his feet, his chest still in agony, as if in a vise. He couldn't run. He could barely walk.

Williams opened the passenger door of his car, stepping around it to let James in. "Please. I promise, it will all make sense."

James watched the android disappear down the road leading up to his house. The moment had passed. He had not done it. He'd let his father's killer go, practically blessed him to . . . James climbed into the black car. The seat was flat and warm and too reclined for comfort, but James made no move to adjust it, keeping his hands clasped, elbows on his knees, breathing steadily now.

"Why shouldn't I kill you?" he asked, when Williams climbed behind the wheel.

"Oh, James, where to begin . . ." He turned the car around, and they slowly climbed the hill. "The time machine, its jumps are preprogrammed. It brought you here for a reason."

"To kill Rene? You?"

"To make the attempt, yes, and then to let him go. Within the hour, Rene will have killed your father, kicking off the chain of events that leads you to find the time machine on the moon next year. The sequence has already happened for you, and as I am an integral part of it, shooting me would create a paradox, which—"

"What do I care?" James said.

Williams's hands stroked the steering wheel as he took a turn, taking them higher into the hills.

"Your father's death is inevitable, I'm afraid. He is too involved in the situation for you to put a dent into his life course. No matter what you try, the sequence of events shall be preserved. He will die, and you will pursue Rene Robertson to the Peary-I moon base where you will find the flying saucer and attempt to stop your father's death. To no avail."

James shook his head as he watched the dry scenery pass by, bringing him closer to where he'd left the machine. "That can't be right. I'm fucking traveling back through time. My actions must influence *something*."

Williams nodded. "That much is true. You may not be able to save your father, but the death of Thomas Brown-Allen is an unfortunate casualty of . . ." He held up his hand, as if disinterested in the end of the sentence.

James's blood boiled at the gesture, at the disrespect. James studied the wrinkled face, the snow-white hair and eyebrows, and the dark stubble of the man who had orchestrated this whole mess. What was he hiding? A lot, probably. But more pressingly, why all the mystery around what had happened? And then it struck him—Williams wasn't worried about the past, because for him, it was still the future.

He doesn't know.

James glanced out the window and said, "You crashed a shuttle into Peary."

Williams was quiet for a long moment, and then he let out a sigh. "Is that so? That is unfortunate."

"I'd fucking say. Right into the main dome, too."

Williams turned his head, his gaze burning through James's head. "You better stop talking, Mr. Mason, lest you tell me more."

James studied that face—old, tired, but also angry and . . . disappointed? The realization of what he'd just done washed over him like a cold shower. In a small voice, James said, "Yeah, right."

"No matter, James," Williams replied, more reserved now as the vehicle rolled to stop at the shoulder next to the dust path James had taken earlier. "Your path is laid out before you. Solve your father's murder, and you will find your answers. But here? Today? You've played your part."

"I'll be the judge of that," James said, fingers on the door handle, itching to get out.

"My apologies," Williams said, and he put his palms together. "The next jump will take you back to the moon, to finish this."

"I'll save Tom and then I'll kill you," James said through clenched teeth.

Williams put out a hand, and James shook it lightly. "I've known you for so long, James. You've saved my life as many times as you've attempted to take it. I can only wish you good luck." He produced James's gun and handed it over. "Don't forget this."

"Fuck you."

Gun in hand, James got out of the car, and it took off with a puff of dust, its matte body barely reflecting any light. James took a deep breath and started down the path toward the flying saucer. In the far distance, his father's Grasshopper craft came in for a landing.

CHAPTER 17

———

James stomped off the yellow dust as he ascended the ramp of the saucer, warm sunlight following him inside. The gun shook in his hand as he paced the deck of the flying saucer, leaving faint footprints, now and then glancing out the viewscreen onto the plain below. The ramp hissed shut.

"How did it go?" the computer said.

"It didn't."

James tossed the gun into his pilot's seat, and it slid across the vinyl into the storage compartment, dropping in with a clank. He stood by the viewscreen, one hand on its cold metal, the other brushing his hair back. He needed a shower. He needed some sleep. His heart pounded against his chest, and his head pulsed as images from that day—*today*, impossibly—replayed in his mind. James, his old 2125 version, was at that moment patching up the robot's hand, the same one James had just shot, while Tommy sat in the lounge, throwing over shy looks that James caught every time. Caught but played dumb, teasing. Later, *after*, neither of them would have the energy for games, and when Tom would move into the villa—with his constantly drunk, way-too-comfortable mother—they would fall not in love but into a mutually beneficial rhythm of sex, cuddles, and words of support that never quite managed to bring relief. Perhaps, given more time . . .

The next jump, Haywood Williams had told him. He could still save Tom. If not here, then back on the moon. And his father? If his death had brought James up to the Peary base, if today had led to James and Tom getting together, then perhaps it was all worth it. Still, he had to see it through, had to get to the bottom of it. Fate had picked old Frankie Mason to merely be a catalyst in these events, perhaps. He'd lived a life rich in all ways, and now he'd done his part, kick-started the events of the last year, and James kept them intact, all in the span of a couple hours. All that was left was to ask Rene Robertson the question again.

"Time travel is not as I imagined it," he said.

"No?" Magpie sounded off, her tone genuinely interested.

"No. It's exhausting and . . . these jumps, they're preset, right?"

"They are."

James turned around and stumbled to the pilot's seat. "Then what do you do?"

"I initiate them, calculate the desired time-space location . . . I also keep the Traveler comfortable and—"

"Right, good," James said, strapping in. "Initiate the next one, and let's go home."

He brushed his hair back once again and wiped his hands on the pants of his overalls as the low hum filled the deck. His eyes closed for a long moment, and then he forced them open. Time trickled as James listened to his own tired breathing, flexing his fingers and wiping his sweaty palms on his pants. Before he could ask the question, Magpie said, "Almost done, James."

He grunted but waited, and then he held his breath, a fraction of a second before reality around him shifted and the view switched from the sun-drenched Santa Barbara to the blinding blackness of space. James breathed. Was this how space looked back on the moon? Kind of, but not entirely—here, the sky was not just black, but splattered with stars, white and with shades of pale yellow with some life to them. His heart pounded again.

"We're still on Earth," he said, more to himself than the computer. "Why the fuck are we still on Earth?"

The machine did not reply, but James did feel it tilt slowly and level, and the viewscreen revealed a mountainous horizon, outlined against a yellow halo of light pollution in a faraway city or town. James all but ripped the harness off his chest and lunged out of the pilot's seat, banging his fists on the transparent metal of the craft.

"Why the fuck are we on Earth?"

Below, moonlight painted the desert a dirty brown with a single dirt road drawn on the patchy canvas. The saucer lowered gradually, adjusting its route, and the computer still remained silent.

"Where are we, Magpie?" James said, looking absurdly at the ceiling, as if the clunker would look back. "*When* are we?"

"May 5, 2125."

James frowned, glancing back at the desert below. "Yesterday. The night before . . . Where are we? 'Cito?"

"Esmeralda County, Nevada."

James stared at the metallic ceiling, his body swaying with the saucer's adjustments, his knees bending slightly. In two strides, he reached the pilot's seat and grabbed the gun, shoving it into his belt. "Get me down."

"Working on it, James."

He walked up to the ramp and shuffled in place, wiping his face and brushing back his hair.

"Can you go any slower? Fuck . . ."

Before he knew it, the interior of some sort of hangar filled the viewscreen around him, and ahead, an unknown source filled it with white light. His right hand caressed the gun.

"Good luck out there," Magpie said, and James cursed under his breath.

The ramp hissed and lowered slowly, and he was walking down before it touched the ground. He shielded his face with a hand as he took a few steps and stopped in the middle of the ramp. When his eyes adjusted to his cold dusty surroundings, James recognized an army truck of some description in the distance as the source of the light. Closer, spread around on the cement floor of the hangar, pale men in black trench coats stared at him. Some handled wooden crates while a few simply stood in place, arms hanging along their bodies, watching. And then, standing on the yellow line at the entrance to the hangar, James saw two figures enter. He recognized them instantly. Carmen, the woman he saw at the Spaceport in Florida, stood next to . . .

"You fucking lied to me!" James yelled at Haywood Williams, his sweaty hand struggling to get a grip on the handgun. "You promised me, you piece of shit!"

Squinting against the light, James managed to get the gun out and swing it upward, its muzzle swaying in a figure eight.

"Why?" he begged in a small voice.

Williams stared, and then mumbled something James didn't care to hear. James closed one eye, aimed, and fired off a few rounds at random. In a fraction of a second, his eyes focused on Carmen, her body shielding Williams. One shot grazed her cheek as more found her body. He saw the figures stagger back, but then the men in black crowded around the ramp, two of them tackling James, knocking air out of his lungs.

Carmen cried out, and the sound echoed in the hangar and rang in James's head as it hit the ramp.

"Please! Dad!"

James wanted to answer her, to say she would be all right in the end, but the words got stuck in his throat. His vision blurred, and he struggled to suck in a breath as cold hands grabbed his arms and legs, dragged him into the flying saucer and laid him down on its cold floor. Blurred, pale faces moved in his vision, cold and emotionless, deathly in the shades of their hats.

Metal clung as a compartment opened, and then James was carried and gently lowered into it onto a soft mattress, it seemed. He stirred, but the compartment closed, and he found himself in a cubby filled with a dim yellow light, with no way to open the lid. At last, he managed to take in a few breaths of cool, sweet air, and he cracked open his eyes, listening. Dull footsteps echoed above and subsided, and then motors whirled, and the ramp hissed shut. They were gone, and he was left in the sleeping cubby. He knew what he needed to do—get out there, get the gun, and finish the job. And then get to Tom . . . and to his father . . .

He stirred, rolling onto his side, his eyes trying to focus on the metal of the wall and never quite getting there. He just needed a few minutes to think, to rest . . .

CHAPTER 18

———

The thin pillow vibrated lightly under his head, and James was pulled from sleep, coming to in his sweat-drenched, itchy overalls. His sleep had not been restful, and he found himself sore and disoriented, the way one does whenever they wake up in a new place—utterly lost and confused. He felt the lid of the sleeping cubby some twenty inches away from his face and took in the subdued light.

"Can I get out now?" he said in a hoarse voice barely louder than a whisper.

"Indeed," Magpie's ever-present voice replied.

The lid didn't open, but the bed lowered into the craft's hold, and James hopped off. The lower deck was a cool, tight space lined with metal—a five-foot-wide corridor that went around the central column, which James assumed contained whatever powered and propelled the machine. He put a hand on the wall and felt it hum and click.

"You better have a shower onboard, Magpie."

"Second door on your left," the computer said.

Circling the hold, he stepped out of his overalls and shook off his undershirt and pants. The cubby combined a shower and a toilet, which under the circumstances was convenient enough. James stepped out ten minutes later and found another sleeping alcove with a similarly ascetic mattress and two lockers.

"When are we?" he said as he got a change of clothes out of an unmarked locker.

"November 21, 2120. Vallesvilles, France."

Clenching his jaw, James slammed the locker door and kicked it with his bare foot, yelping in pain and crashing on the mattress. He cursed, rubbing his toes. November 21, 2120, was *six years ago*. Where was he then? Around this time, his father had left his post as the CEO of Bastion Security but remained the owner. He'd practically retired without losing control of the company, and he and James could afford to leave San Francisco and come to live in 'Cito. James met Tom a year later, in high school. They'd been friendly but never that close. He wondered if Tom even knew his name at this point in time. He cursed again.

"Is this bad?" the computer said. "I can't help but register your elevated vital signs and—"

James wiped his face. "It's fine." He considered asking her why this year, why France, and what the hell Williams expected of him, but then . . . none of it mattered. In the end, he dressed in black pants and a long coat and picked a slim backpack out of the dented locker. The time machine had taken him further back into the past, and for the first time in the last day or so, he felt optimistic. It had gifted him with five more years to prevent his father's and Tom's deaths, five more years to track down and kill Williams. He had time to prepare.

Further down the circular corridor, he found a storage room filled with the same wooden crates he'd seen the men in black handle in the Nevada warehouse. Most were unmarked, but on some, printed in block letters, he read *Providence Foundation.*

"What's in these?" he asked.

"Supplies, I believe, for your travels."

James scoffed. "Fat fucking chance." He went past the storage alcove, swinging the backpack on his shoulder.

"Proceeding with the mission is imperative, James," the computer said as he neared the ladder that led to the deck.

"I am," he replied. "But none of this time travel business for me, thanks. I'm exactly where I want to be, and I've got everything I need."

He climbed the ladder onto the deck and shut the lid behind him, shaking his hands as he observed the tight space. The viewscreen showed only the night around the saucer with a few distant lights. Discarded near the ramp, he found the gun and twirled it in his hands, looking for a way to load it. It appeared to be chiseled out of a solid block of some metal with few moving parts apart from the trigger, and even those he couldn't get to open. But then, as he gripped it, a full bar highlighted just above his thumb. *Energy-based, then. Neat.*

He stuffed it into his coat pocket. Before going, he had one last thing to check. Knowing the answer, he said, "Hey, Magpie, can you call my father? Frankie Mason?"

Without a pause, the saucer replied, "Not at this moment, James. The integrity of your mission at this point depends on discretion and—"

"Oh, fuck off. Open up."

The ramp hissed open, and James walked out into the night, zipping the coat as he did so. The late French fall met him with cold air and a thin layer of snow crunching under his boots. He stood in a field illuminated by the flying saucer's interior light, and visible in the distance were a few lights of a town. All around, the horizon was low and even, with only some trees and country houses here and there. The saucer itself was wedged comfortably in a copse of naked trees in the middle of a field, its hull completely invisible.

Behind him, the ramp hissed and closed, and James was left alone in the white field with little to go on but the light in the dark. So he walked. Stepping briskly on the frozen grass, he crossed the field and reached a one-lane road lined with lights spread far apart and a small town on the other side of it. James walked across the pavement and into what was barely a town—a main street with a few dozen low homes spread around it. A couple of people were out on their evening walks, or maybe headed home from a bar, and everyone James passed gave him the kind of look an outsider gets when passing through a tight-knit community. He smiled and nodded, but his right hand gripped the gun in his pocket.

He spotted a restaurant in the distance—a wooden hut mostly hidden under a layer of snow with an inviting neon sign above the canopy and a porch swing next to the entrance. There, a slick maroon sedan rolled to a stop just as James was about to duck inside. Two women stepped out of the vehicle, both dressed in identical brown pantsuits, white collarless shirts, and white homburg hats to match. James froze. They eyed him and moved with purpose to where he stood.

The younger woman, who had stepped out of the passenger seat, said, "James Mason?"

He took an abrupt step back and tugged the gun out of his pocket, and the other woman, the driver, unbuttoned her coat with one swift movement.

He said, "Who the fuck are you?"

The passenger, holding her gloved hands up, eyed the gun and said, "Agent Olivia Farewell. We're on your side, James."

She didn't offer a smile. *Farewell.* James said, "My side?"

"Hungry?" She lowered her hands. "How about we get some food and talk about it? Come on."

With that, she went into the restaurant, leaving James pointing the gun at nothing.

"You should probably hide that," the other woman said, inviting him to go in. "Don't wanna scare the locals."

James stared at her a long moment, but then he did put the gun away. Whoever they were, dealing with them out in the cold would not be ideal. His hands were beginning to freeze, and his stomach rumbled. One step at a time.

A few minutes later, the three of them sat around a wooden table covered with lined cloth, putting away bread and butter and chasing it down with red wine. They were the only patrons in the rustic establishment, but they still grabbed a booth in a far corner. In the lights of the eatery, James saw Olivia Farewell was a year or two older than him. She wore her red hair short, and her eyes constantly watched James as if expecting him to bolt at any time.

The older woman said, "Would you like to take your coat off, James?"

"I'm good," he said, taking a drink. "What's your name again?"

"Lauren. Lauren Farewell."

He glanced between the two. "So . . . is Farewell, like, a family operation?"

Lauren pursed her lips.

Olivia said, "It isn't, but that's beside the point. We're here to provide your orientation."

"Orientation? Thanks, I'm fine on my own."

Olivia sat back in her chair and clicked her thumb and index finger twice, and her fingertips produced a small holographic screen. James's eyes widened.

"You are the son of Frankie Mason, presently residing in Santa Barbara, California, correct?" He nodded. "CEO and owner of Bastion Security, yes?"

"Get to the point, okay? I need to get going."

Lauren took a sip of wine, watching him as Olivia scrolled through her file and said, "Looking into your father's activity will be a challenging mission for you, James. The service Farewell provides might make it easier. New identity, money, perhaps even specific intel to aid you in your investigation. Interested?" She finally smiled, and the screen in her hand flicked out.

James considered it. He had no plan, not really. Nothing concrete, beyond somehow flying to California to let his dad know what was up. He'd need to stay quiet, under the radar as much as possible, and if that didn't work, he'd send an anonymous message. Come to think of it, Olivia's resources would sure come in handy there.

He said, "Who do you work for? Haywood Williams?"

She shook her head. "I'm not at liberty to discuss that, James, but no. We have no affiliation with Dr. Haywood."

As Olivia spoke, James watched the older woman. Lauren seemed distant and almost disinterested in the conversation, enjoying her dinner instead. In his mind, he recalled her hand unbutton her coat outside, no doubt ready to reach for a gun. Whoever these women were, they had to be more than messengers.

"Tell you what," Olivia said, "I'll give you five minutes to think this over, okay? Excuse me."

She stepped away from the table then, leaving him and Lauren to share the rest of the wine. James chewed his bread and washed it down. He couldn't help but wonder what would happen if he declined the offer, if that was even an option.

As soon as Olivia Farewell was out of view, Lauren said, "Finish your drink."

"Huh?"

"Go on, drink." As if to lead by example, Lauren emptied her glass and got up, putting on her hat and coat. "We need to go."

"I'm not going anywhere with you."

With a small sigh, she whipped out a gun identical to his own, the one he had stolen from Carmen. Could she have been a Farewell too? Lauren aimed the gun at his face. "You better move it. Now."

Almost choking on his food, James finished the wine and got up, his chair shrieking on the wooden floor. He went outside, and Lauren followed him closely all the way to the car. "Get in," she said, and he climbed into the front seat.

Once she was behind the wheel, the vehicle purred to life, and the doors locked.

"What the fuck is this all about?" James said.

Lauren turned the wheel and stepped on the gas, saying, "Olivia lied to you."

CHAPTER 19

———

Lauren sped down the main street of the town, the name of which James had already forgotten, the car's wheels tightly gripping the shimmering winter asphalt. James held the gun in his lap, remembering the woman he'd encountered in Florida yesterday and then shot out in Nevada. Carmen. Her uniform had hardly resembled the pantsuit-and-hat combo of Lauren Farewell, but then, maybe it was a French thing. Or a future thing.

"You've got some explaining to do," he said. "Do you by any chance know Carmen? Or Adelia Farewell?"

Lauren shot him a sideways glance. "Can neither confirm nor deny."

"Right. You said your—um, partner?—was lying?"

"She is and she was." Lauren pressed a button on the steering wheel, and the driver's seat slid back softly and turned to James at an angle. She flicked the overhead light on, creating a cozy atmosphere. "Olivia was . . . well, full of shit." She took a deep breath, looking past James out into the night. "Okay. Farewell, the organization we work for, is affiliated with Haywood Williams. I don't know the details, but my understanding is he gives the orders."

James clenched his jaw, hand tightening on the gun.

Lauren continued, "Don't look at me like that. I'm on your side. For real. Dr. Williams is dangerous, and your dad's outfit, Bastion Security? They work for him too."

"Impossible." James tried to sift through vague memories of his father's work engagements, but not a single connection came to mind. Frankie ran a private security company that protected businesses all over the West Coast, so theoretically he could've serviced Williams or one of Providence Foundation's many subsidiaries. He said, "That would've come up during the trial, right?"

"What trial?" she said.

James threw back his head. Of course, the trial. The trial, which would happen six years from now. He said, "Never mind that. Still, no way my dad worked for Williams."

"Maybe not directly, but Bastion has dozens of subdivisions and affiliates, as does Providence." She gave him a moment to connect the dots. "You know how I know all that? One of those affiliates, Trident Armaments, provides Farewell with gear."

James glanced at the gun in his lap, its dark brushed metal shimmering ever so slightly. In all his life, James had never seen his father show any interest in guns. Frankie, for all his faults, had been more interested in the finer, safer things—comfort, convenience, technology. But business would be a different matter. James tucked his gun into the backpack he had in the footwell. Out of sight. The car cruised at a steady speed, the aura of its high beams illuminating the lonely road lined with a rickety wooden fence and the ghostly fields on either side of it.

"Why are you here?" Lauren asked. "Whose trial did you mention just then?"

"This robot, Rene. He killed my father. Well, he is going to kill my father a few years from now. He's still alive, though. So there's your answer. I'm here to learn what the fuck happened to him."

She nodded. "That's correct."

James waited for any other reaction. When it didn't follow, he said, "You're awfully calm for someone talking to a time traveler."

A smile touched her lips. "I've been briefed, you know. Part of the job. You are a curious character, James, I'll give you that. So your father is still alive, so that's good. Your mom?"

"The briefing omitted the part where she died when I was a toddler?"

She hid her face in her hands and shook her head. "I'm so sorry, I . . . yes, the briefing did omit that. We're only getting information relevant to your mission."

He clung to the words. "There are other missions? Other time travelers?"

"Not in my experience. You're the first time traveler I know of, but yes, there are other missions. Extraction, cover-ups, that sort of thing." She shrugged and watched him expectantly.

"Where are you taking me, Lauren?" He looked into her bright hazel eyes and saw a mix of determination and something else. Maybe fear. They sat in silence for a few seconds.

"You tell me, James," she said. "The car's on autopilot, just floating along." When he didn't reply, she said, "Here's the deal. I can help you. I have intel. I have resources. We can find your father and prevent his death."

"And how is this different from what Olivia offered?" James said, turning his seat to face her. "What's in it for you?"

Lauren crossed her arms, once again glancing into the darkness behind him. "I'm thirty-six. Still a junior agent, for all intents and purposes, driving around teenagers like I'm their mom, echoing their words so they sound more convincing. I've got to get out of this cycle, James."

"So why not quit?"

She snickered. "Let's just say the agency doesn't exactly provide a retirement plan, if you know what I mean." And then, after a moment of silence, she added, "I just ditched my partner for this. There's no way back for me, James. Let me help you."

He drummed his fingers on his knee, weighing his options. It seemed Lauren was familiar with the protocols of whatever bullshit scheme Williams had engineered. The agents had found him in the middle of nowhere, precisely at the right time. And if she were as resourceful as they'd boasted, then it could certainly make things easier. *New identity, money, intel . . .*

He turned the seat back to face the windshield. "We need to find the time machine."

"Glad you mentioned that," she replied as they turned off the road. The car elevated its clearance and gripped the snow-covered field.

A few minutes later, they rolled to stop next to a familiar copse of trees. Even with the high beams, there was no trace of the flying saucer, and for a brief moment, James's heart skipped a beat. If the damn thing had gone on without him . . . well, he could work with that, especially now with Lauren on the team, but he didn't like their chances. They'd be forced to work as fugitives, most likely, going against Farewell, the men in black, and whatever other temporal safeguards Williams had at his disposal. It seemed, whatever

James tried to change, Williams would be there to fix or prevent altogether, which left him with pursuing the truth about his father's death.

The engine fell asleep, the lights still illuminating the trees, and Lauren put her hand on the door handle. "Ready?"

They stepped out, and James swung the backpack on his shoulder. It seemed he'd left the saucer days ago and returning to it now felt like coming home after a long holiday. He reached out, feeling for it and flinching, expecting to bang his head on its hull. Was it even there? His heart pounded.

And then the car's lights died, and they were left truly alone in the coldness of the night. *Fuck. What now?* James turned around slowly, his eyes still adjusting to the dark, searching for Lauren's silhouette. She stood a few feet away, frozen.

"Agent Farewell," Olivia said, and both James and Lauren turned in the direction of her voice. "What do you think you're doing?"

Olivia's form separated from one of the trees, and she stepped forward. Outlined against the shimmering snow was her gun—the same shape as the one James had in his backpack. Lauren raised her hands, and he did the same.

"The asset was a flight risk, yeah?" Lauren said. "Well, he tried to flee."

"Is that so?" Olivia stepped closer, gun still trained on her partner. "No wonder we're on High Alert protocol. They warned me about you, Lauren. You're somewhat of a scary story back at the academy, actually."

"Am I?"

"Oh, yeah. More of a hindrance than a help out in the field and questionable convictions. I can see why now. How quickly do you think they'll promote me once I bring you in?"

James watched Lauren take a slow, deep breath, and it dissipated in the breeze. The next moment, she lunged forward, her hands enveloping Olivia's gun. Shadows danced, and after a metallic *smack*, Lauren emerged with the gun turned around in her hands. Olivia stumbled backward, slipped, and landed on her ass, one hand clutching her nose.

"That's right, *Agent Farewell*."

James lowered his hands. "We need to go, Lauren."

"In a minute," she replied, and she stepped up to Olivia. "This will give you a story to share." And she pistol-whipped her partner, knocking her out cold.

"Now can we go? Just leave her," James said. He stepped away, once again feeling for the flying saucer in the air.

Lauren didn't follow. Instead, she put away the gun and picked up Olivia off the ground. The car's door swung open as they approached, and she loaded her partner into the driver's seat. The engine whizzed to life, and Lauren shut the door.

As she caught up, James reached out in the air in front of him, and his hand touched the ice-cold metal of the craft.

"Open up, Magpie."

After a moment, the machine hissed and cracked open, white light spilling seemingly out of thin air, snowflakes dancing in the beams. Snow crunched as the ramp touched the ground, and James led the way onboard. He dropped the backpack into his pilot's seat, claiming it, and watched Lauren join him on the deck. The ramp closed, and she stood by the exit, looking around.

"You'll need to take your shoes off," James said.

She held his gaze, and then reached down to undo her shoe.

"I'm joking, Agent! Come on in."

She breathed out and stepped on the deck, walking up to the second pilot seat, because there was nothing else to walk up to. James gestured at the lid he'd emerged from earlier that night. "All amenities in the hold below," he said. "Feel free to explore."

She gave a short nod and put her hat on the second pilot's seat. "I will. What's our plan?"

"We need to look into Bastion. I need to find out what my dad was up to. Hey, Mags, where's the next jump taking us?"

"Welcome back, James," the computer replied, and Lauren gave him a quizzical look. "We're going to Toulouse, France. Twenty kilometers west of here."

"No way," Lauren said. She leaned on the chair, staring intently at the floor.

James said, "When?"

Before the computer could speak, Lauren said, "Three years ago, isn't it? The Toulouse chapter of Farewell, *my* chapter, had a breach three years ago. That must've been us!"

Magpie said, "That is correct. We'll be arriving at Toulouse on November 17, 2117."

"That must be how we learn about Bastion Security," Lauren said with a sparkle in her eyes.

Her sudden enthusiasm unsettled him, but James had to smirk. It seemed Williams had a point. No matter what he did, James could no more back out of the journey than he could walk away from Magpie. And if there was a path to learning about his father's past, he would take it.

"Fine," he said, taking the gun from the backpack and storing it in the pilot's seat. "Let's strap in and get the hell out of here. We can figure out a plan when we get there." He shot his copilot a look. "I'm counting on you."

Lauren gave another short nod and climbed into her seat, tucking the hat away. They both put on the harnesses, and Magpie said, "Initiating the jump. Calculating time-space coordinates."

Lauren said, "Is there a pill we need to take?"

"Take a deep breath"—she did—"and breathe out . . . now."

They both did, and then, as if a switch had been flipped, night changed to day, and the sun, reflecting off the ground outside, blinded them. They were no longer out in a field, however. When James's eyes could see again, he realized that shimmering outside wasn't a blanket of snow at all, but water. They were parked on the bank of a river, tucked underneath a bridge and looking out on the water, dark but not frozen over. Across the river, a three-story brick building hung over the bank and a taller, ten-story glass tower glistened in the sun above it.

"November 17," Magpie said. "Toulouse."

"*Merde*," Lauren whispered. "We're in the past."

"Don't get your hopes up," James said, and he unbuckled his harness.

CHAPTER 20

———

"This is it," Lauren said, slowly getting out of her chair, her eyes glued to the viewscreen. She took a couple swaying steps toward the transparent wall. "The Farewell HQ. Are we really in the past?"

"Indeed," Magpie replied. "Three years ago, for you."

"Nine years in the past for me," James added. He lingered in his seat, watching her and the outside. A tiny paranoid voice in his brain informed him that her fellow agents were probably outside, waiting and laughing. But Lauren had her back to him, and his hand was on his gun. In the end, he slid out of his seat and stepped away.

"Let's see," she said, joining James at the hold hatch. "This means Olivia and I, in this time, are away on training in Paris in preparation for some mission. I'm showing her the ropes, if you can believe it. Boy, what a spoiled little thing that one is . . ."

James climbed down the ladder and found the storage alcove. Lauren was at his side moments later, and they hauled a crate out that said *Tech Supplies*. The men in black had loaded other crates there, but now was not the time to explore. Lauren produced a multi-tool out of one of her hip packs and pried it open. Inside, James found a small faux-leather box containing a bracelet similar to the one he'd gotten on the moon.

"You said something about a new identity? Can you work with this?" he said.

She grabbed the bracelet, inspected it, and with an "aha" showed James a little logo on the strap. "Trident Armaments," she said. "I've been using these my whole career."

She grabbed the bracelet and put it on her wrist next to her own Trident device. A couple taps on it, and a screen materialized, which Lauren scrolled, swiping lines of text in the direction of the new bracelet as if dealing cards. When that was done, it came to life, blinking a blue light. Lauren handed it off.

"Nice to meet you, Alan Rosenbaum." They shook hands, and she added, "I also cloned my Farewell access codes, so we should be able to go in without an issue."

"Neat." James put it on and hid it in his sleeve. She seemed pleased, but the convenience sent off alarms in his brain. "Anything else useful in your briefing?"

Lauren shook her head. "We're freestyling here, James. This is three years ago, remember? I didn't even know you existed."

James himself would be thirteen, living with his dad in their old house in Seacliff, San Francisco. They'd go to the movies on the weekends, and sometimes, on the weekdays, Frankie would take him to the office after-hours. His dad would work, and James would roam the empty spaces, exploring the environment. He was fascinated with empty workstations, each personalized with photos and trinkets, cups of coins and dried-up coffee. In those days, James never bothered to ask what his dad was working on so late—he didn't need to know.

And now, the only person who could tell him was this strange woman, dressed to the nines and armed with an energy handgun. Lauren's intel—or whatever they'd find at this so-called Farewell HQ—would be a handy clue to make the next step easier. Unless Williams was behind it all, leading him on this wild mission through time. But he had too little of that time to waste on philosophical musings on the nature of free will. The breach was happening today, so they had to get moving.

Back on the main deck, as James—Alan Rosenbaum—and Lauren were gearing up to leave, Magpie said, "One more thing before you go."

"What's that?"

"A moment . . ." And then that same voice came out of his wristband. "We're good to go, James."

He and Lauren exchanged a look. "Did you just upload yourself onto the comm?"

"In essence, yes. My computational ability is hindered by the hardware, but my consciousness is portable. I'll be linked to the craft, too."

They walked out into the chilly November day, and the ramp snapped closed behind them. No agents to meet them, no ghostly men in black. James breathed in fresh, sweet air off the river and blew out a cloud of fog. Lauren did the same, and they climbed the snowy slope away from the water, crossed a strip of frozen lawn lined with naked trees, and found themselves on *Quai de la Daurade*, a narrow two-lane street that stretched along the embankment. Lauren led the way as they passed parked cars and turned onto the bridge to cross the river.

"Nervous?" she said.

"Nah," he lied. "Whatever my dad was into, I need to know. You?"

"No. I'm liking this feeling. It's like we're invisible, isn't it? Nobody knows we're here. Nobody's searching for us." She looked out over the river, its green waters rippling in the cold breeze. A boat passed silently below, a silver needle cutting the water without a sound, and the people onboard waved. Neither of them returned it.

"You're not getting away, are you?" James said. "Are you looking for someone here?"

She sucked in a breath. "My younger . . . sister. You?"

"There was. But they're okay, for now." Tom would be twelve and living with his mother.

The words hung in the air, and then the moment passed, and neither of them pressed the other. They crossed the bridge in silence, and up close, he saw the glass building was actually part of the older brick structure, growing out of it like some shimmering animal that had shed its skin. They stopped at the end of the bridge and leaned on the railing. Lauren watched the building while James stood half-turned, casually.

"It used to be a hospital a long time ago," she said. "Technically, it still is one on all the paperwork, doing mostly research—which isn't entirely false, either—with branches all over the globe. I hear there's one on Mars even."

James grunted. The idea of Williams's tentacles stretching throughout the solar system gave him chest pains. "Are you sure we can get in?"

"Yeah. I haven't gone rogue just yet." She gave him a wink and jerked her head, and James followed her off the bridge and toward the building.

They entered the territory through an inconspicuous checkpoint—a booth with a scanner that Lauren lightly touched for it to buzz the fence open—and then crossed the small inner park dominated by a marble statue of a woman surrounded by benches and bushes. As they passed the granite base, James read, "Dr. Eveline Farewell." If they really were a family, it was a big one. Neither of them commented, and they walked to the set of revolving doors below a long line of French words. *Hospital* was the only one James recognized.

They entered a clean but cold lobby with rubber mats at the entrance and a wide reception desk that reminded James of every hospital he'd ever been to. Both stomped their feet, leaving blots of snow on the pristine mat, and Lauren scanned her bracelet once again to get through the ceiling-high turnstile. Behind the desk, a single young woman in a white coat worked the computer, paying them little attention.

"Lauren Farewell."

The receptionist glanced up, then pushed a button. "Confirmed," she said with a slight accent, and then frowned at the screen. "Aren't you supposed to be in Paris, Agent?"

"Had to return early."

The woman studied them, and the pause made James sweat. He became aware of the silence in the lobby—no phone calls, no chatter, no personnel moving down the hallways.

Finally, Lauren said, "This is Dr. Rosenbaum."

She stepped aside, and James stretched out his wrist and then pulled it back. The receptionist checked with her screen and gave them a nod. "Go ahead."

James followed Lauren down the hallway on the left, and when they were out of earshot, said, "That was smooth."

"We have maybe twenty minutes, *Alan*, so keep up."

She quickened her step, and he did have to catch up to her to match her pace. "Why?"

"During that training mission in Paris, the one my past version is at right now, I'll be summoned for a random credentials check. So maybe twenty minutes, maybe fifteen, maybe less."

They walked briskly down the hallway and took several turns, getting progressively deeper into the facility. Lauren had taken off her hat and carried it on her chest with her left hand, her right one hanging freely at her side. James could imagine her reaching into her coat at any moment, and he tried to formulate a plan of his own. The gun weighed down the right pocket of his own coat but getting it out had proven rather difficult. Chances were he'd be shot before he even touched it. Unless he shot *through* the pocket—

"We're here," Lauren said. James bumped into her.

She scanned the wristband, and a door opened, letting them into the archives, filled with rows of buzzing machinery. James followed Lauren through the maze until they arrived at a terminal diagonal from where they'd entered on the corner of two rows that let them observe the passageways. Lauren tapped on the holographic screen as James watched her navigate the outdated archival system, sifting through folders and hidden lines of code.

"There he is," she said, "Franklin Simeon Mason."

His father's file was short, barely a few sentences. He was listed as the owner of Bastion Security, parent company to, among other things, Stealth Impact and Trident Armaments that provided, as Lauren had said, weapons and accessories to [redacted].

"Is that it?" James said. "We knew all this."

"I don't understand," Lauren whispered, sifting through more files and double-checking her searches. "This is the most secure database in the whole building. It should be here."

"Maybe it's a clearance thing?"

She glared at him. "No, it isn't."

She checked again while he watched the maze, expecting the security—maybe that of his own father—to storm the room and drag them out. Nothing happened.

Lauren sighed. "It's useless. There's nothing. Either it's been erased, or it's kept somewhere else."

Blood pounded in James's head. They stood, looking around the room as if waiting for the terminal to change its mind and gift them with something more substantial, and then Lauren shut it off.

"May I make a suggestion?" Magpie said on James's wrist.

He brought it up. "Yes!"

"The schematics I have on file for the Toulouse branch of Farewell suggest there is another archive in the building."

James stared at the wristband and then at Lauren. How the computer onboard his flying saucer had the information was beyond him. Well, not entirely. "Take us there," James said.

"Of course," Magpie replied, and a small map appeared over the wristband, leading them out of the archives. "Also, according to your calculations, Agent Farewell, you have seven minutes before the alarm is raised."

James was walking before she finished the sentence, following the red line on the map. Behind him, Lauren said, "If there's another archive, one I didn't even know about, then I definitely don't have the clearance to access its files."

"Can you hack into it, Magpie?" James said.

"That would be difficult. The archive in question is not digital."

With Lauren's codes, they passed through multiple locked doors, and James had to hide the map when they passed a security guard in the inner lobby of the building. This one offered no pretense, and the white hospital interior was replaced by rather drab stone walls and colorless carpets on the floor. Palms in white pots guarded the corners and white benches to match crowded the space. A couple of women drank coffee on one, and they gave Lauren polite nods that she returned.

"Are all Farewell agents women?" James whispered as they entered the stairs.

"You catch on fast, Time Traveler."

"Said the junior agent . . ." James pushed open a door of the B3 level, and they took another hallway that ended in an unmarked wooden door with a simple lock for an actual metal key. James pulled the handle. Nothing.

"Let me," Lauren said, and she pushed him aside, getting close to the door.

He heard the clang of her multi-tool and then a snap, and the door swung open. They invited themselves into a dusty cement basement lined with crude metal shelves held together with bolts and nuts and sagging under the weight of countless boxes of file folders.

"How much time, Magpie?" Lauren said.

"Two minutes, thirty seconds."

They split up and searched folders, which was made harder because there seemed to be no logic to their place-ment—no alphabetical or subject matter order that James could discern. He sneezed more than a few times, and sweat filmed his forehead after a minute of pulling out cardboard boxes and rustling paper files, most of which were gibberish, like random coordinates and code words, redacted names of people and places, and dates going back to the 1990s. As he dug through the trash, he heard Lauren curse under her breath. A box marked *armaments* caught his eye, and James pulled it, ripping off the cover. His heart raced as he read the markings on the folders inside: *Rampant Technologies, Levels, Bastion Security.*

"I think I found it," he said.

Lauren hurried over, her steps dull in the cramped space as James pulled out the folder. Inside, slimmer files contained information on the entities affiliated with his father's company, including Stealth and Trident. James flipped through them until he found the main *Bastion* file. He skimmed it. Most of it was information he knew already—his father's place of birth, current residence, children. But then he read:

Wife—K. C. "Casey" Mason, deceased.

Previous alias Casey Farewell.

He scanned the line a few more times, as if forcing the words to change, trying to process them. "This can't be right," he said, barely above a whisper.

Lauren snatched the file and scanned it. "Casey Farewell. Holy shit. I think I've heard the name, years ago."

"What are you talking about?" James said, still in a half-trance.

"Your mom was a Farewell agent, James. And if I were a betting woman, I'd say there's more to her death than whatever you've been told."

James stepped back, letting the box of files drop to the floor, and leaned on the opposite shelf. "I never knew her," he said. "Not even—"

"Security has been alerted to your presence," Magpie said. "They are en route."

Lauren whipped out her gun and grabbed James by the elbow. "Tell me later."

CHAPTER 21

———

Lauren pulled him away, and James stumbled over the spilled files on the floor, almost slipping but grabbing onto a shelf to steady himself. She shouldered the rickety door and led with her gun to the staircase, and he followed.

"How do we get out?" James said into his comm.

"The facility has a number of underground passages not included on any official blueprints," Magpie replied. "You will need to get to level B1, like this . . ."

The map floated above his wrist, and Lauren studied it for a few seconds. James did too, but his panicked brain, not yet fully recovered from the revelation about his mother, couldn't make sense of the red lines twisting in the 3D space of the map.

"Let's go," Lauren said. "And get your gun out, for fuck's sake."

With a shaking hand, James did, holding up the smooth weapon as if he'd never held it before. "I don't want to kill anyone."

"Neither do I. Here." She put a hand on the barrel and tapped it in a few places. "Hold it tight now."

James did, and the gun morphed to perfectly fit his grip. After another quick tap, like magic, the barrel grew sights on the top and an additional laser pointer on its side. Blue letters right above his hand spelled out *stun*.

"Good to go."

They ran up the stairs, scanning the space with their guns but not meeting resistance. On B1, Lauren stormed through the door, and James saw her let out a couple quick shots. When he entered the hallway, two women lay unconscious on the floor, their guns next to them. Out of reflex, James pointed his gun at the sprawled shapes, but then Lauren leaped over them and ran, and he tried to catch up.

"Where to next?" she called.

"Second door on the right, I think."

She slammed into it, but it didn't give, and scanning her wristband resulted in the door letting out a screech and blinking red. "Shit. They know where we are now."

"Third door. I'm sorry!"

That one turned out to be unlocked, and they rushed through it and found themselves in a research lab of some sort containing metal tables and armchairs with integrated machinery—scanners and sensors of some kind. A few people in buttoned-up lab coats raised their hands as Lauren ran past them, and James stayed close, waving the gun around, mostly for show. Through the lab, they entered a narrow backroom cramped with boxes and more machinery under canvas tarps. James blocked the door with one, and they went on. The room ended with a bare wall, and Lauren felt around its edges while James stood watch, gun pointed back the way they came.

"The map shows a passage behind it," he said. "A tunnel, I think, which should lead us to the surface."

"Any idea how to get in?"

His wristband stayed silent. James strained to focus, taking deep breaths as he stared at the holographic map so conveniently uploaded into the bracelet. "Wait," he said. "Williams is behind it all, right?"

"Not the best time for conspiracy theories, James."

"I'm just stating facts. Those crates in the flying saucer? Williams's men in black got those onboard."

Lauren turned to him, her gun pointed at the floor. "And?"

"And it contained the wristband, which paired up with the AI, which just so happened to contain the map of his place that even you didn't have."

"Whatever you're getting at—"

"The jump to Toulouse was preprogrammed like all the other jumps, too, and the fake ID you encoded into this can't be random, either."

She watched him, and then she nodded. "It was the ID we were supposed to give you, yes." And she stepped aside, saying, "Work your magic, then."

James stepped up to the wall and traced a rectangle with his wrist, waving it in random patterns until something on the other side beeped, clicked, and then a six-foot-high panel sank into the wall and slid aside.

James beamed at Lauren, but she pushed past him. "Let's move."

There weren't many other options, so they ran down the narrow, low tunnel, illuminated by occasional strips of dim white lamps built into the ceiling. The map blinked, showing they were still below the building, moving toward the river.

"You see anything?" he yelled.

"Not yet."

The next moment, a hand shot from behind a turn, and Lauren was knocked back, the gun disappearing in the shadows and clanging on the floor somewhere. She went down hard, grunting and rolling as she clutched her chest. Two men in black—the same pale androids in hats—stepped into the tunnel, blocking the way out. James aimed the gun at them, the laser sight jumping between their chests, but the robots showed no reaction, inching closer.

"I'll fucking shoot you. Stay back!"

They didn't, and James shot the one on the left with zappy blue bursts that did no damage at all. James barely registered the other robot jumping him, and the next moment the gun was out of his hands, replaced with sharp pain, and the android delivered a swift punch to his face.

***

"You okay?" Lauren said in a low voice.

James swayed in the back of a car, breathing through his mouth, his eyelids weighing down his whole head. He blinked them open and focused on the soft, spotless upholstery. He tasted blood.

"Don't move your face too much."

He couldn't. The slightest twitch felt like another punch. Sitting up, James discovered neither he nor Lauren were restrained in any way, and the androids sat silently in the front. They drove down an empty two-lane road squeezed between two fields, much like the one in the town James had left a few hours ago. James brought up the wristband. "Mags? Can you get us out of here?"

One of the androids glanced in the rearview mirror as the comm device said, "I can't. My signal is being jammed."

"Right." He looked back at the driver. "Where are you taking us?"

Lauren replied for him: "To their boss, I gather. Dr. Williams? Why not just kill us, huh?"

No comment from their captors, but James agreed with Lauren. The car, he noted, was identical to the one Williams had picked him up in on the day of his father's murder, eight years from now.

"Is my face bad?" he said.

"I don't think it's broken, just messy."

He noted that she even had her hat on, though their guns had been, of course, confiscated. "How about you?"

She touched her chest. "This will leave a bruise. I've seen limited AI, but these assholes give the word a new meaning. Could've asked us nicely first."

James smirked and immediately regretted it. He used his sleeve to wipe his nose gently, and he brushed back his hair. The men in black largely ignored them, so he got comfortable, watching the white fields dotted with trees and farmhouses swim by.

"You said before," Lauren started, "that there was someone, you know, out there. In the future."

"Uh-huh." James kept looking outside. "And I'll go back to them, alright?"

"You don't have to tell me. I just thought . . ."

James didn't say anything, but he reached into his hip pack and brought out the little velvet box, crusty with blood. He weighed it in his hand, went to open it, but stopped. Now really wasn't the time. Lauren didn't say anything when he put it away, and they rode in silence for a long while.

Soon the fields got lonelier, with few homes in the far distance and black trees lining the road like barbwire. The car turned off the highway onto a private road. They drove for ten more minutes until the road morphed into a well-kept alleyway walled by evergreens, which led them to a massive wrought-iron gate. James and Lauren popped their heads between the front seats to get a better look at the large, gilded *W* enclosed in a wreath.

"Williams," James said.

Lauren sat back. "Wish they hadn't taken my gun. What now?"

James tried to breathe through his nose to no avail. "I'll talk to him. He'll listen to reason. Maybe he'll even tell us what's next for us on this fucking mission . . ."

The gates opened, and they drove through and up the winding driveway past more evergreens. The alleyway brought them to a wide three-story chateau as white as the snow surrounding it, and the car stopped in front of the entrance. The men in black stepped out without a delay and opened the rear doors, letting in the cold wind. Lauren held on to her hat as she climbed out. The courtyard opened onto a sprawling field with a perfectly rectangular ice-skating rink a few hundred feet down the slope. Around it, wooden structures like barracks stood covered in a thin layer of snow. A few people were skating while some carried chopped wood into one of the buildings.

"What's that about?" James said.

"No idea."

Without words, the androids led them into the chateau. They entered the bright white-and-gold foyer made entirely of marble and wood, illuminated by a crystal chandelier that gave off cold, unwelcoming light. As they looked around, the men in black exited, like shadows unable to take the brightness of this new space. James touched his face, stepped on the worn carpet at the center of the foyer, and put his hand on the white piano, leaving a smear of blood.

"Ahem."

They turned to see a young woman watching them from the hallway on the left. She wore a black-and-gray dress that ended at her knees, her hands in the pockets. The little hat on her head had a small holographic bird flapping its wings.

"Welcome, Mr. Mason," she said. "And you, Agent Farewell."

James took a few steps in her direction and, putting on his hard-ass voice, said, "Where the fuck is Williams?"

The woman's lips curved in a somewhat amused smile. "I wouldn't know."

"Then why the hell are we here?"

She watched his eyes, and then glanced down at his nose. "I suggest you watch your tone, Mr. Mason. It is my understanding that rash decisions tend to get you in trouble."

He grunted but took a step back. The woman was slightly older than him, with a focused, intense face framed by short black hair. "If you follow me, please." Her heels clicked on the stone as she went past them and up the marble staircase, hands still tucked in her pockets.

James gave Lauren a look, and they followed the hostess. Upstairs, they walked past more gold, wood, and marble and framed maritime art until the woman stopped at a tall set of doors.

"Remember my advice from earlier."

James opened the door, and they stepped into an office starkly different from what they'd seen before. Thick curtains kept the windows impenetrable to light, and despite the tall ceiling, the room was dim and cozy, with a few subdued lamps spread around on the desk and cabinets at the walls. A silhouette sat in a grand armchair in the corner, reading a book, and she shut it when James and Lauren entered. They stood at the doors, waiting.

"Well, well," the woman said in a raspy voice. "Fancy meeting you here, isn't it?"

She set the book on a side table, got up, approached them barefoot, and stopped at the desk, putting a hand on it. She was a beautiful woman in her late forties with cold eyes and lines in the corners of her mouth, and there was no hint of a smile there. Her maroon dress was not dissimilar in style to Lauren's uniform, and her blonde hair just touched her shoulders.

"Holy . . ." Lauren whispered. "You're Ekaterina Fortepianova. Dr. Williams's wife. What are you—"

"Not just Haywood's wife, Agent Farewell. To you, it's Director Fortepianova."

Lauren gasped but didn't say another word. The head of Farewell stepped closer to them.

"Listen," James said, "I'm sorry that we broke into, whatever you call it, your HQ here—"

Fortepianova raised a hand, and he went quiet. She measured them with her steely blue eyes and said, "Quite a fuss you made in Toulouse, Mr. Mason, I'll admit. And you, Agent? That's one way of getting on my radar." She leaned on the edge of her desk. "Decisions need to be made now, yes?"

The tone of her voice made James listen, his own thoughts shrinking in her presence.

"If I may," Lauren said.

"You may not." Fortepianova drummed her fingers on her chin. "Your transgression is punishable, but, I suppose, to preserve the integrity of the timeline, we can let it slide. Your . . . current version, the one who's out in Paris, will not get reprimanded. It simply wouldn't be fair to hold back such a talented student, yes?"

Lauren nodded, but James said, "Integrity of the timeline? You're in on Haywood's bullshit, too?"

"I am, Mr. Mason," she said without a pause. "We are family, after all, and this"—she motioned around with her fingers—"is somewhat of a family business." He only frowned, so she shrugged and added, "Families, Mr. Mason. Surely you understand." A knock came from another room, short and rapid, and she said, "Not now, dear."

But then the door burst open and a girl no older than ten ran in, carrying a little flower in her hand. Her hair was longer and her face softer, but James recognized it instantly. Young Carmen, her face smiling and bright. He swallowed, squinting his eyes to stop tears forming.

"Here, mama, this is for you!"

Fortepianova took the flower, and when the girl hugged her waist, she put a hand on her shoulder. "Thank you, dear." She smelled the flower. "Carmen, did you pick this from the bouquet in my bedroom?"

The girl grinned. "Maybe . . ."

James watched the scene in disbelief. A moment ago she'd been deciding fates, and now she played a mother to her daughter. But then the director glanced his way, and her face again turned serious. Those steely eyes saw right through him. She said, "What is it, James? Speak up."

"Carmen?" he said, addressing Fortepianova. "She's Haywood's daughter, isn't she?"

"She is. What of it?" Was it concern he saw in her eyes?

The girl looked at James, confused and a little scared. He said, "You are so dedicated to Williams's vision of the future, Director. Do you know he is willing to sacrifice your daughter in the name of it?"

In a tone devoid of emotion, the woman said, "Carmen, go to your room, dear. Mama has to talk to her guests." The girl hurried away, and Fortepianova put the flower on the desk. "What are you talking about?"

Steadying his breath, James paced the room as he constructed his next lie. He couldn't know how much of the future the director knew, but her reaction seemed genuine enough. If he played his cards well, the lie would pay off. He turned around in the corner and watched Lauren and the director waiting for his next words. "Carmen might make a fine Farewell agent one day, I have no doubt. That's the plan, isn't it? I know a thing or two about plans, Director, and let me just say, 'Man plans, Haywood Williams laughs.'"

"Get to the point, Mr. Mason," she replied. She stood rigidly at her desk, listening intently with her arms folded.

He walked over and sat on the guest side of her desk, giving his shaking legs a rest. He breathed out. "About two days ago—well, about eight years from now, on one of my first jumps—I meet Carmen and Haywood, and he lets me kill her. She jumps in front of him and goes down. I'm sorry."

It was Fortepianova's turn to pace her office, first back to her armchair, and then to the locked window. "You are bluffing."

"Are you putting it past him, Ekaterina?" James put his elbows on the desk, lacing his fingers. "Would that be the most awful thing he's done?" He glanced back at Lauren and gave her a wink.

At the door, Lauren poured three glasses of whiskey from a crystal decanter and set them on the desk. James put a hand around his tumbler as Fortepianova walked over.

"Well," she said, "that does change our arrangement."

James raised his glass. "Families, Director Fortepianova. Aren't they a bitch?"

CHAPTER 22

———

Ekaterina Fortepianova emptied her glass and slammed it on the desk. She took a step away from them. "I can't believe he would—*is* going to involve Carmen in this." She glanced at the door her daughter disappeared through. "This was the line we agreed to never cross . . ."

James sipped his drink, studying the finer details of the office: the texture and the wear of the mahogany desk, the organized chaos on top of it, and the director's bare feet below, toes pinching the carpet. He waited for her to marinate on this new information, to draw some of her own conclusions. And then, before she could dissuade herself from flipping over to their side, James said, "I'm sorry, Ekaterina. What happens to your daughter, it's in my past. Nothing I can do about it—"

She silenced him with a hard look. "I don't need a lecture from you, Mr. Mason. I know how this works. Rest assured, I'll deal with Haywood. He's not going to see Carmen ever again."

He couldn't look away from the fire in her eyes. "Thank you. I cannot stop him, but maybe you can help us with something else."

Fortepianova glanced at Lauren and lifted her empty glass. Lauren refilled it. "Thank you, Agent." She took a sip, savoring the aftertaste this time as she watched the dark liquid swirl. She said, "You have strong-armed me into a favor, Mr. Mason, but this path you are on . . ." She shook her head. "It ends in misery and disappointment. Trust me, I've been on that path most of my life."

All three of them finished the drinks, all satisfied and a little relieved, and James said, "The worst has already happened to me, Director. Now I need to find out why. Will you help us?"

She clicked her fingers together like Olivia had done, and a holographic screen materialized above the desk. They couldn't see through it, but the director typed, saying, "I'm being told you broke into the old archives in Toulouse. Find anything interesting?"

"My mother," James said. "The file we found called her Casey Farewell."

The director nodded recognition. "Ah, Casey, yes. She was a fine agent."

James swallowed. It was true, then. He tried to remember anything, any small detail his father had told him about this woman, *Casey Farewell, Casey Mason,* or whatever the hell her name had been. College sweethearts, he'd say, in Santa Barbara, in fact. Married young, back before Frankie had a business to speak of. Had a child, whom Casey hadn't gotten the chance to raise. And then . . . nothing. They'd never talked about mom. James had never met her, so the concept itself had always seemed abstract and alien to him, and now it turned out she'd had this entire life before he was born, one full of intrigue and espionage. There were no pictures around the house, no belongings in abandoned boxes in the garage.

His father had flings now and then throughout the years, but never anything serious. Now James could understand why.

He said, "Dad told me Casey died a couple years after I was born. Some illness. Is that true?"

The director didn't need to consult her screen. "No."

James banged a fist on the desk, and the tumblers jumped, and Lauren flinched. Fortepianova didn't. "What happened to her?" he said.

"I'm assuming Agent Farewell has enlightened you as to the nature of our job. It is conducted in secret, and it remains a secret. One doesn't get a happy retirement in the end." She glanced at the screen. "Casey's death was made to look like an accident, but I can't tell you much beyond that, I'm afraid."

"I think you can," Lauren said, crossing her arms, a touch of a sly smile on her lips.

The director's face, illuminated by the screen, seemed pale and static, unblinking. "Agent," she said, "I can make your life very difficult, you know."

"But you won't. You haven't."

She bared her teeth in triumph, and James had to mirror it. Their future was untouchable now, even to the director of a secret spy agency, or whoever they were. It was their past. It had happened already and . . . and then it dawned on him and choked the victory. Lauren gave him a look of pride that quickly turned into concern and then anger as she understood.

It was Fortepianova's turn to grin, and she got up from behind the table and grabbed their glasses and headed for the decanter next to the doors. She only poured one glass. "Won't I, *Junior* Agent Farewell? Haven't I?" she said. "How long have you been stuck in that rank? I'm guessing twelve years? More, I suppose, seeing as how you are from the future."

James saw Lauren flex her hands and pull at the skirt of her coat. She wasn't crying, but she wrinkled her nose in an incoming outburst.

He said, "We'll fix it," and put a hand on her knee. "Don't let her get to you."

James glared at the director, who leaned on the minibar, tumbler in hand, and watched the two with patient curiosity, as one would observe animals in a zoo. She took a sip of whiskey and licked her lips. "Casey Farewell died twelve years ago, in 2105, in San Francisco. Her flyer malfunctioned as she was leaving a meeting, and, unfortunately, the impact of the crash killed her instantly. Our agents assisted the police in recovering the body."

James hid his face in his hands, taking it all in. His father had never shared much about his mom. What had he known about her? Was he part of it? James looked up at Fortepianova, searching for something, *anything*, in her face. Pity maybe or understanding at least. But she simply watched him, not blinking, standing at the door as if hinting it was time for them to leave.

"Why?" he said. "Why did you kill her?"

She raised her hands in defense. "I had nothing to do with it beyond giving my blessing, Mr. Mason."

He wanted to feel the loss, to feel robbed and orphaned. He wanted to hate her for these words, for so casually talking about his mother's death, but he didn't. Because then, she said, "I would've ordinarily, but this matter was handled by security."

Lauren turned, and she and James waited for what they both knew was coming next.

Fortepianova took a breath, lowering her hands. "This path you're on, it will not bring you peace."

"Just say it."

"Bastion Security. Franklin Mason gave the kill order."

James jumped to his feet. "Can I save her?"

She shrugged. "That's my husband's department. My work is more grounded." He looked into her eyes, and for the first time her face betrayed emotion. "Based on my experience, the answer is no. But . . . maybe you could see her."

His heart pounded in anticipation as he brought up his wristband and tapped it. "Magpie, what's our next jump?"

"You will be traveling to San Francisco, California, September 2, 2105."

James glanced at the director, and she said, "That's the day, Mr. Mason. A car is waiting for you downstairs."

He nodded to Lauren, and they left the office a bit too quickly and without a goodbye. James walked down the hallway tunnel-visioned, as if the building was on fire, and Lauren kept up. "I wanted to kill her," she said.

"I know, but we can't. Not here, not now. We need to go back."

In the foyer, Fortepianova's assistant waited by the front door with a man in black next to her. She didn't smile, and they ignored her, storming outside. As promised, the car waited in the driveway, its rear doors open with another android in a black fedora standing guard.

"I'm sorry about your mom," Lauren said on their way back to the flying saucer. "That is no way to go."

The sun had set recently, and the sky, covered with a blanket of clouds, was light gray and slowly shifting. Rare snowflakes flew by the car, and James tried to keep track of them but quickly lost count.

"Everyone I loved died—were murdered."

Lauren didn't speak, and James didn't know what to add. He'd gone through life without a care in the world. No reason to be afraid or angry, really, beyond the trivial. It seemed life had been happening while he was . . . what? Wasting time in the garage with the fucking sailboards? His dad had killed his mom, and to top it all off, they'd both been secret agents working for Haywood Williams. Where did that leave him?

And Thomas. The only person who had been there, who had really tried.

He reached into his pack and brought out the little velvet box Tom had gifted him. It seemed to burn his palm, and James took a deep breath before finally opening it. The little enamel pin blurred in his eyes, and James pinched the bridge of his nose, breathing out. The blue flower still had a smear of dried blood on it.

"What's that?"

James showed her the pin. "A keepsake."

She took the box and turned it in her fingers to catch some light. "It's pretty. This must've been someone special."

James chuckled, looking out the window. "You know the saddest part? I don't even fucking like irises . . ."

She returned it, and James clipped the pin to the lapel of his shirt and shut the coat, discarding the bloody box on the floor. They drove the rest of the way in silence, and when the men in black let them out on *Quai de la Daurade*, they walked down the slope, snow crunching under their feet.

"Hey, Magpie, you can start your calculations," James said as they entered the saucer, "but let us get some sleep before you initiate the jump, yeah?"

"Understood," the computer replied.

"Thanks." He hovered between the pilots' seats, and Lauren stopped before going down into the hold. He said, "Thank you for doing this with me."

"Thanks for letting me tag along." She started down the hatch, stopped halfway, and added, "Um . . . do you want a hug or something?"

He smiled, climbing into his pilot's seat. "Maybe later, when this is over, yeah?"

CHAPTER 23

———

The hatch popped behind him, and James startled awake to the view of the river covered by night. A few boats passed back and forth. The opposite embankment, lined with street-lamps, was dominated by the Farewell HQ, checkered with random office windows still in use. In the dark, the newer part of the building was almost invisible, leaving bright rectangles to float above the old brick building. Lauren joined him in the copilot's seat and handed him a tumbler of coffee. She wore a white long-sleeved shirt and the same pants she'd had on before.

"Slept well?" she asked.

James stirred and sat up in his chair, adjusting his clothes, and then took a sip. "I slept, so that's something. You?"

"A little. I kept thinking about the director's words, about our path and all. She's the one, James. She keeps me in the lowest rank for the rest of my life."

"It's 2117, right? Where would you be if it weren't for Farewell?"

She glanced out the viewscreen, cup nestled in her hands. She didn't turn back as she spoke, "I'd be thirty-three, probably still living in upstate New York. I'd play guitar. I was pretty good in high school. I could've been in a band or played solo."

"And why didn't you?"

She looked away. "My parents sent me to the police academy. Sort of a family thing. From there, I got pulled into Farewell." She paused, tasted her coffee. "It seemed exciting, this spy life, but . . . I would've rather played guitar."

James nodded along. "My dad played when I was little. I always wanted to learn but never bothered, and now I'm in my twenties."

Lauren said, "You should start. You know, life's long. Had you started then, you'd have had fifteen years of practice."

She had a point. He'd rolled back nine years in the last few days, and yet he felt nine years older. Time moved in the same direction. The coffee was bitter, but the smell made up for it. He said, "So guitar. What else?"

"I'd be driving my mom's old Ford, top down, traveling around the country without a map, looking for the simpler times, just . . . being. Instead, I'm in Paris, reading a bunch of crap about time travel with my teenage partner. Did you seriously think we were a mother-daughter team?"

"That was the old me," James said as he emptied the tumbler and, before she could protest, hopped out of his seat. "I'm gonna go change, and then we can make the jump, yeah?"

He went down to the hold, took a quick shower, and then picked out a fresh set of clothes from his locker, not forgetting to transfer the lapel pin to the fresh shirt. The men in black had returned their guns as well, and he found a holster in one of the supplies crates and clipped it to his belt.

On the deck, Lauren was geared up and already strapped into her chair, and James took his place next to her.

"We're ready, Mags," he said.

The viewscreen went blank, and the machine initiated the jump. James and Lauren inhaled. Seconds later, they found themselves breathing normally again, and the wall went transparent, greeting them with a magnificent view of San Francisco: glass towers rose to the sky, their tops lost to the clouds, and the green balconies and gardens gave the city an otherworldly verticality, as if mother nature had reached up and wrapped itself around the towers, decorating and bridging them. Flying craft buzzed between buildings like so many organized worker bees. James had visited once on his father's business trip, but back then, the architecture didn't impress him.

He climbed out of the pilot's seat and walked over to the edge, putting one hand on the transparent wall to steady himself as he glanced at the world below. They'd been parked on top of one of the towers, tucked away between the building's roof and its landing platform.

"Why are we here, do you think?" Lauren said, and he turned to face her.

"We're here to see my mother."

"Yes, but where?"

"Nothing about these jumps is an accident, right? My parents lived in San Francisco, but further west near the beach. So why are we in the business district?"

Lauren unbuckled her harness and hopped off, joining him. She studied the skyline, then pointed, her finger pressing against nothing. "There. Providence Foundation."

James focused on a tall tower with several levels of gardens and a lower one next to it, connected by tunnels on multiple levels. "Shit, you're right." He paced the deck, circling the two pilot seats, one hand tapping their backs. "Bastion Security, Farewell, Providence . . . they're connected, and they all work for Williams. My mother must've found something she wasn't supposed to, and he had her killed."

Lauren watched him, and then she said, "Do you mean Haywood Williams or your father?"

He threw her a knowing look. *Either. Both.* Did it matter at this point? Still, he needed to be there, to see it with his own eyes. He needed to find his mother.

Lauren offered, "Maybe she wanted to retire, to start a life with your father. To raise you."

"Maybe. Maybe she went to make a deal with Williams and that didn't go over well. Ekaterina said today was the day. If my mom was—is here, at the Providence Foundation, then that's where we'll find her flyer. We need to get there before she does and stop her from getting on that transport."

Lauren gave a short, professional nod. "I think I can help with that."

The saucer let them out, and they went around and found their way to the landing platform above. Protected by air walls, the platform was quiet and calm as they walked between parked vehicles.

"I've been trained for this kind of op," Lauren said, ignoring James's sideways glance. "Extraction, too." They stopped at the edge of the platform. "The West Providence Tower is the main one," she said, pointing at the taller skyscraper. In an op like this, you'll have watchers on the closest nearby rooftop as well as agents on the ground to swoop in and clean things up."

"So we need to stay in the sky," James said, eyeing surrounding flyers.

"But we need to be quiet about it. We can take the bridges here, here, and there." She gestured at the green tunnels connecting several towers, including the one atop which they were standing. The last time James had been to the city—more than ten years in the future—the skywalk had been expanded into the city's upper level above the clouds, but now only a few bridges covered in trees and shrubbery connected the tallest towers, all leading to Providence Foundation.

"Let's go."

A few minutes later, an elevator let them out at the bridge, and they crossed it, brushing elbows with a couple office workers on their breaks, and found themselves in an open-plan space with computer monitors and people in headsets waving their arms in the air. No one paid them attention, and they crossed the floor and then another bridge. In this tower, the skyway forked, with two tunnels leading to other buildings.

"Let's split up here," Lauren said.

"West Providence on the left. I'll take that," James replied, and he put a hand on her shoulder. "Be careful, okay?"

"Put the gun into kill mode, James," she said. "And if you see Casey, tell her I'm sorry."

Before he could answer, she took off, her figure disappearing into the sunlit green tunnel, low palms and flowers swaying in the breeze. There was no time to follow her.

James took the other tunnel, and once he reached the West Providence, he found an elevator that took him to the third floor from the top. There, he ducked into a dimly lit staircase, leaning on the cold wall to catch his breath. He fidgeted with the holster and took out the gun, sliding a finger on the barrel to put it into *kill* mode. The word blinked red. Imitating what he'd seen Lauren do, James swept the stairwell as he climbed the steps, holding the weapon with both hands. With his heart threatening to punch a hole in his chest, he was just crazed enough to actually shoot someone this time. He stopped at the top of the stairs and listened through the door. If his parents were on the other side, there was no sign of it—only the whistling of the wind. James took a step back, braced himself, and stormed through the door.

"Hands up, all of you!"

When his eyes adjusted to the sunlight, he found the landing platform almost entirely vacant. Red lights blinked on its perimeter, and a single flyer was parked at the edge a hundred feet away, unguarded. The model was an expensive one, its hull polished and shimmering in the sun. James approached it slowly, gun aimed at the door, thinking of all the things he could say if his mother was inside. Thirty feet out, the door slid open.

"No," James mumbled.

A man in black stepped out, pale as a ghost and holding on to his black fedora, trench coat flapping in the wind. Behind him, Haywood Williams looked out with a sly smile on his face. Another android stepped around the vehicle, and they flanked the old man.

James's finger itched on the trigger. "Where is my mother?" he called, gun trembling in front of him, but less than before. This time, he liked his chances of hitting the target.

"Ah, that's right. That's why we're here, isn't it? To prevent your mother's death." Williams nodded, hands folded in his lap. "You're not going to use that gun, are you?"

"Maybe I should."

"You should, but do you? Have you? In the future you're from, have I been shot and killed today?" He paused, and the corner of his mouth twitched. "History will preserve itself, James."

"So you've told me."

"Yes, many a time." Williams waited, and James lowered the gun. The whole time, the android bodyguards stood without movement, hands on their hats in a comical mirror image of one another. "Come here," Williams said, "and you'll have your answers."

James stood there for a long moment, not sure what to think. Was Casey Farewell (or Mason) in the flyer already, waiting for him? Was she already dead? He stepped forward, his right hand still wrapped around the handgun. "Speak."

Instead, Williams gestured with his hand off to the side, and James realized he was pointing to the East Providence Tower, a few hundred feet away and some stories below. Its landing platform was likewise empty except for a single flyer—a common civilian two-seater, pearl-white.

James's left hand shot up to his mouth, and he said into the wristband, "Lauren, come in, are you there?"

But the band remained silent.

Williams said, "It appears you've been tricked."

"What the fuck are you talking about?"

Moments later, a few figures appeared on the other platform, two male, one female, with one of the men leading the woman by her elbow. She stumbled, blindfolded by a black hood over her head. For a terrifying moment, James thought he was leading Lauren, but the woman's clothes did not match. Instead of the pantsuit, she wore a green jumpsuit with a black belt. One of the men was an android, dressed in all black. The other James recognized immediately. His father, Frankie Mason—younger, leaner, with a clean-shaven face and slightly longer hair than he would wear in the future.

"Casey Farewell," Williams said. "An agent too capable for her own good."

James was vaguely aware of the tears rolling down his cheeks, and when his vision got blurry, he blinked and watched his father lead his mother toward the flying craft. She struggled, kicking and wriggling. Frankie lost his grip on her arm but quickly regained it, and James saw his father make a swinging motion around her neck.

He pulled. Hours seemed to pass as his father strangled her, until his mother's body went limp. Frankie didn't let it hit the ground but carried it into the flyer and shut the door. In the meantime, the man in black was half-inside, fiddling with the controls. James wanted to do something—to shoot at his dad, or maybe turn and shoot Williams in the face, but he was transfixed, some deep morbid part of his mind anticipating what came next.

"What did she do to you?" he choked.

"Is there an acceptable answer? Agent Farewell got too close to me, that's all. She started poking in places she should rather have stayed out of. She should've stuck to her job."

Williams stood with his arms crossed and watched the scene with James. The flyer on the other rooftop took off smoothly and headed away from the city. Seconds passed, and it lost altitude and then spun out of control until it disappeared from their view. James jumped and then backed away from Williams, raising the gun as the muffled *pop* of the crash echoed through the skies.

"I'm ending this," he said.

The old man didn't even turn to look, and then one of the androids grabbed James's wrist, its metal fingers wrapping around the wristband, cracking it and tightening like a vise. Instinctively, James pointed the gun at the robot's chest and pressed the trigger twice. Bolts of energy shot through the man in black like knives through butter. He collapsed.

Without thinking, James pointed the muzzle at the other approaching guard and shot him dead. Both robots now lay on the platform, motionless, their hats blowing lazily in the wind.

"Impressive, Mr. Mason." Williams turned. "It's an honor to be here for your first kill. Or your last? It's a matter of perspective, I suppose."

"Tired of your bullshit," James said, and he pulled the trigger.

Nothing happened. Not even a noise out of the gun, as if it had bricked in his hand.

That same sly smile crawled onto the old man's mouth. "History, remember? It keeps itself intact."

Enraged, James leaped forward, his gun-wielding hand raised above his head, aiming for Williams's face.

The old man's hand shot up and grabbed him by the wrist and pulled his arm down. The gun disappeared from James's hand, and the next moment he was turned around, one arm twisted behind his back. Williams holstered James's gun and pushed him down to the hot tarmac.

"You have done all you could, James, and you got your answers." He got down to one knee next to James. "Your father murdered your mother. Now you have just one thing left to do to ensure this journey of yours takes place."

James blinked, and then he saw Williams offering him a hand. "Fuck off," he said, in a voice less confident than he would've liked.

"Fair enough, James." Williams stood up, shaking off his slacks. "You will find Rene Robertson here at Providence. Yesterday."

Just as Williams started for his vehicle, the flying saucer hissed behind James, and he turned to see the ramp open up, revealing the interior of the invisible craft. Lauren ran down the ramp and over to him, her heels clicking.

"Are you okay?" she said.

Williams's flyer took off silently and was gone. With Lauren's help, James got up, wiping his face as they headed for the saucer. "We've got a robot to find."

CHAPTER 24

——

"Strap in," James said as soon as the ramp shut and they were alone on the deck.

Lauren hopped into her seat. "I'm sorry, James. I didn't get there in time, and when I realized what happened—"

"It's fine," he said through clenched teeth. "It's happened. It's done."

"I got Magpie and we came for you as quickly as we could."

"I noticed," he replied, and then he took a deep breath. "And thank you."

He put on the harness and got ready to give the order, when Lauren said, "What . . . what happened there?"

Through the viewscreen, he still saw the landing platform his mother had left—was killed on—and the image of his father, young, energetic, and purposeful, still lingered in front of his eyes. The man never wavered as he strangled his wife and threw her into a flyer destined to crash. Who was he, that man? He was so ruthless, so cruelly confident. And at that moment, a one-year-old James was left at their little house in Sea Cliff with a nanny, while his parents' secret lives as Williams's operatives had come to their logical conclusion. Inevitable conclusion.

James wanted to call Tom to tell him everything that had happened—about the time travel and the Farewell agency and Haywood Williams and everything in between. He wanted to warn him to stay the fuck away from him and the moon. Of course, Tom was barely born, and calling his mother, well, that would be insane. *Hi, Molly, you don't know me yet, but your future son and I, we . . .*

He shook his head. "Williams happened. And my dad killed my mom. Magpie, initiate the jump."

Inhale. Exhale. Day became night with a flip of a switch, and white spots danced in James's eyes. By night, the living upper city of San Francisco had an unnatural, mysterious quality to it, as illuminated greenery camouflaged buildings almost lost to the night, if not for the reflections of thousands of lights. Flyers coursed between the towers, and a leisurely airship floated high above, tethered to the highest tower.

"We're still here," James said.

Magpie replied, "Relatively speaking, yes. Our geographical location on Earth is the same. Sixteen hours in the past."

James picked up a new wristband in the supply storage, and they snuck out onto the landing platform. Two small black flyers were parked at the edge, both unmarked, and James had an idea who owned them.

"The men in black," Lauren confirmed. "They might be waiting for us." And then she added, "Where are we going, exactly?"

"Rene Robertson is here in the building somewhere. I need to find him."

"The robot who killed—will kill—your dad?"

James inhaled the sweet night air, as they headed for the elevator. "That's the one. I need to finish this. Or start it, depending on your—fuck, I'm starting to sound just like him. Let's go."

The elevator moved smoothly, and they didn't talk until it was halfway down. That's when James unholstered his gun. "It's jammed," he said.

"These things don't jam." Lauren picked it and twirled it in her hands. "I haven't seen anything like this before. It's just dead." She tried to tap the barrel, sliding her fingers in patterns and even pulling the trigger. Nothing.

"Well, let's hope I don't need it," James said, and he holstered it. On the ground floor, the doors opened, and he said, "Magpie. Any info on Rene Robertson?"

The wristband stayed quiet for a moment, and then she said, "My records say a delegation of sentient AIs has been staying at the Providence tower for a few weeks now. Rene Robertson is among the four. You will find them at the lobby cafe."

"Delegation," James muttered. "Thanks, Mags."

He hid the band in his cuff, and they walked through the lobby. At any moment, James expected the pale androids to ambush them or Farewell agents to storm in, guns drawn, but nothing of the sort happened. The high-ceilinged lobby with polished granite floor was empty of people at the late hour, with a single security guard snoozing behind the reception desk. Their steps echoed as they walked toward the cafe—a nondescript little place in the corner of a lobby with a little plaque next to the door and a neon coffee cup above it.

Rene Robertson and company were the only ones there, sitting around the largest table at the place, all with steaming cups in front of them. Rene hadn't changed since the last time James had seen him, twenty-one years from now. He wore the same white shirt, and his tan jacket was folded on the back of his chair. Three other Buddhist androids, two men and one woman, also were in the same clothes. Standing out from the crowd was a woman dressed in a violet business suit. Her dark hair was done up in a bun, and she stared at James.

"Rene, can I speak with you?" he managed to say.

The android looked up with recognition in his face, as if he'd been expecting the late-night guests. He apologized to his companions and excused himself, putting on his tan hat on the way out to the lobby. "James," he said, as the three of them stepped through the door, "is everything okay?"

James studied his artificial face, so unburdened and sincere, and said, "No, it's not."

The android took a closer look first at James, and then at Lauren. "Agent Lauren Farewell?"

"Um, do we know each other?"

"Oh." Rene offered his hand for a shake. "You must be early in your journey, yes? My name is Rene Robertson. James and I are old friends, though he doesn't know it yet."

Lauren shook the hand, and James thought the robot sounded truthful. There was an air of joy about him, of lifted spirits and anticipation. If James waited any longer, Rene would undoubtedly invite them to have coffee with the rest of the delegation. If he waited any longer, James would break down.

"Lauren," he said, "could you give us a moment?" When she nodded and stepped away, he turned to Rene. "We've only met a couple of times, Rene, in your future, which is my past."

The android nodded, still in anticipation, but the joy drained from his face, and the half-smile turned into a half-frown.

James steadied himself, ignoring the rising pain in his chest. "You said we were old friends? I'm glad to hear that.

Now, Lauren and I don't have much time, and I need a favor to ask you."

"Yes. I'm ready."

James took a good look at Rene, at his clothes. The standard-issue shirt, pants, and hat, all symbols of a simple, clean philosophy the sentient machines subscribed to. Some called them Zendroids, at peace with the world. They were pilgrims, living on the road, studying the planet and all there was to absorb and internalize.

James said, "Twenty years from now, in my home in Santa Barbara, I want you to . . . to kill my father."

Rene's face twisted with horror. His nostrils flared, and his lips parted, but then he composed himself, and he put a hand on James's shoulder. "Absolutely not."

James grabbed the android's arm and said, "I know what I'm asking is horrible, but you must listen. I'll tell you what happens . . ."

And he did, giving the android just enough details of his father's murder to paint a picture without revealing too much of the future in the process. For all James knew, Williams would tell him on that car ride to Montecito, anyway.

Rene listened, and then he lowered his hand off James's shoulder. "My friend. You are asking me to take the life of a man I've never met. I know Haywood torments you, and I feel for your struggle. But some things I cannot do for you."

With that, Rene stepped back inside the cafe, leaving him alone. James stood at the door, watching Rene join his companions at the table as if he'd never left. They talked, and the woman in the purple suit listened. Perhaps that was it, then. He'd failed. The android refused. James considered following him inside, talking to him again to make sure he understood, but then, it had already happened. Whether it was fate or some physical equation, his father was dead, would be dead, when and how James had witnessed it happen. There was nothing else he needed or wanted to do here, in this time. So he walked off.

Lauren was pacing just outside, and James caught the tail end of a conversation: "Please, answer!" When she saw him, she lowered her wrist a bit too abruptly.

"Who were you talking to?" he said, innocently enough.

"I can't say."

"I understand if it's your sister, Lauren, it's fine. Trust me." He stood next to her in the chilly breeze. "Take your time. I'm in no hurry anymore."

"It's not that . . . ugh." She couldn't stand still, wringing her hands and shuffling in place. Finally, she broke: "I lied to you before. But now that we've . . ."

He could come up with a few ways to finish the sentence. Too exhausted to react, James simply listened, leaning on the cold glass of the lobby windows.

Lauren said, "I was trying to reach myself. The younger me, the present day me, the stupid twenty-one-year-old junior agent me."

James looked at her, and the dawning realization made him tap his foot, and his mouth went dry. All he could do was shake his head, even as his mind replayed their earlier assault on the Providence Towers. *If you see Casey, tell her I'm sorry.*

"It was my first big op," she said, her eyes wet. "I didn't know what the fuck I was doing. I thought I was one of the good guys, doing the job, helping out . . ." Her arms dropped, and he waited for a reaction that never came. "I tried to warn her, I mean myself, earlier, on top of the East Providence Tower, but . . . but I never reached her." She met his gaze.

"But I can fix this. There's still a few hours before the accident, James. I can warn her. I can get to her. I know where she is!"

He kept shaking his head, looking out at the night city and its lights, buzzing vehicles above, and gardens in the sky. It was all there, living, moving, and it would still be there tomorrow, a year from now, ten years. He'd seen the future. He'd lived it. "You can't change it," James said. "It's done. It's happened, or it will happen. I don't give a fuck anymore. We're done here."

She tried to take his hand, but he staggered away from her and planted both feet firmly on the ground. The coldness of the stone was slowly freezing him.

"I was young, James. I didn't know what I was getting myself in—"

"You helped them kill my mother. I should've never brought you along."

He walked off, going back inside and across the empty lobby toward the elevators. Lauren followed him, pleading and making up excuses he didn't bother to catch. At the elevator doors, he stopped abruptly and made a one-eighty. "If you follow me, I swear I'll get my gun to work and shoot you with it. Back off!"

The elevator dinged, and he backed into it, and as soon as the doors shut, he broke down.

CHAPTER 25

———

On the landing platform atop the West Providence Tower, three men in black stood around near their vehicles, watching. James paused for only a fraction of a second before walking out the elevator and heading for the flying saucer. "I know, I know, *or you'll make me go.*" He waved them away. "You can fuck off now. I'm going anyway."

He tapped his foot as he waited for the ramp to lower, and then he meandered up it and waited for it to shut. The deck felt especially cool and empty without another person on it, and even the seat that James had come to think of as Lauren's, which he had previously barely considered, stood abandoned and useless. James headed below deck and shrugged off his clothes on the way to the bed. "Hey, Mags," he said, just to hear another voice in the strange corridors.

"James. Were you successful?"

The words came as a stab to the gut. Had Williams programmed the machine to rub it in? He wondered. "I was, Magpie. Lauren, though, not so much."

"Oh?"

James turned on his mattress. "It doesn't matter. It's done. We're done." He sat on his mattress, slightly trembling. His brain urged him to dig through supply crates to find another gun and dispatch the guards outside. Then he could ditch the time machine and just disappear, get away from Providence and get lost. He could find his dad and Tom in the future. He imagined living as a hermit somewhere for twenty years. He'd be in his forties. What a joke.

He tried, "Is there any chance you can teleport to the future?"

"No chance, I'm afraid. But if I may offer an opinion, James, I don't think you should leave just yet."

"Why's that?" He was exhausted but couldn't get his eyes to shut. The mission was accomplished, but it didn't feel that way. Instead, his mother had been taken from him—for real, this time—and any hope he'd had for a future was ripped away. And he lost the man he thought had raised him, who *would* raise him. That stage persona was shattered, revealing the killer underneath. The past sucked. And Tom? He was gone.

Magpie said, "I think you make a good team, and I believe Lauren genuinely cares for you."

"She's got an interesting way of showing it. Did you know she was involved in my mother's death?"

"I heard as much, yes. For what it's worth, my speech pattern analysis determined she was sincere in her apology."

She'd play guitar, Lauren had said, in a different life, if she'd had the time. Had she not fallen into the Farewell trap. Much like him, she was forced into her mission, and like him, she'd found nothing but misery. Lauren longed for an escape.

"Lauren, come in," he said into his wristband. And then to Magpie, he added, "You're right. I need to find her."

James rolled out of bed and into his clothes, already cold from the metal floor. He didn't bother with the belt and the bricked gun. He climbed and leaped to the ramp as it lowered. At the foot of it, the men in black stood three-wide, watching him with their dead eyes set deep in pale faces—three ghouls waiting for him to step closer.

What am I doing? He said, "Never mind, guys, took a wrong turn back there."

The ramp hissed shut, as James jumped into the pilot's seat. He drummed his fingers on the smooth, shimmering panel in front of him, an extension of the left armrest. "Mags, you can fly, right?"

"Of course."

"Let's try it, then. Get me down to the ground. But before that . . ."

The panel lit up with instruments and all kinds of data that James ignored as he buckled in. He put his hands on the holographic controls, which weren't that different from his father's Grasshopper—tangible holographic throttle levers and a control stick—and slowly turned the craft around, aiming at the men in black and their flyers. They watched as he pushed the throttle, and the saucer crushed them as it slid forward, and then it hit the flyers, brushing the wrecks aside.

"You can take over, now, Magpie."

The flying saucer lifted gently and all but fell off the edge of the platform. Incredibly, James barely felt the force of the motion, as the pilot's seat smoothly adjusted its orientation, keeping him level with the ground below. A moment later, it halted, landing on the empty plaza in front of the building. James stormed out, but Lauren was nowhere to be found. He called for her, and his voice echoed in the night. He brought up his wrist comm.

"Lauren?" There was no reply. His heart sank, cold sweat breaking out all over his body. He watched his reflection in the glass of the Providence lobby, small and translucent in the night. He said, "Magpie, can you trace Lauren's wristband?"

"Working on it."

James muttered curses under his breath on the way up the ramp. The instruments lit up, and a 3D map showed Lauren's location as the saucer lifted off. It traveled through the city, but whatever it used for an engine didn't employ a propulsion system. The effect James got was that of sitting comfortably in a stationary craft as the world around it moved and shifted in some unknowable pattern, as if the saucer was a cog in a giant machine. It sped up until he could no longer keep track of the city, and then, just as quickly, the world stopped, and James half-expected the buildings to crumble.

The saucer lowered into an empty parking lot of some long-abandoned structure. James hurried out and crossed it, stepping around scraggly little bushes that had pushed their way through the ancient concrete. The building itself was likewise derelict—a five-story concrete skeleton put together using massive slabs with dark spots of dampness and more pathetic greenery throughout.

"I'm here!" he yelled, illuminating the darkness of the building with a flashlight of his comm.

Instead of a reply, multiple hands grabbed him from behind, lifting him off the ground and carrying him forward with tremendous speed, their footsteps echoing all around. The next moment, James found himself in a secluded corner of the structure, its floor damp and soft. Remains of furniture rotted at the walls, and what little light there was came from a crack in the ceiling. James turned to see two men in black standing in the hole in the wall that used to be a doorway. He lunged at them, but they pushed him back.

"Why am I here?" he asked, getting up. "Where's Lauren?"

The androids didn't reply, but they did leave the room, and moments later, Haywood Williams stepped through. He wore a jet-black jumpsuit and he leered when he saw James there. The man James knew as one of the most prominent scientists of the twenty-second century stood out in the damp and dirty ruins like a ghost haunting the concrete corridors. His pale face and immaculate silver hair gave him the appearance of a floating head.

He breathed out through his nose and said, "You should know that at one point, it would've given me great pleasure to see you like this, James, desperate and lonely. I would've told you that you deserved it, that karma had caught up with you." He shook his head, as if catching himself. And then added, "You mustn't have slept much in the past few days. I'm sorry."

"Where's Lauren?"

"This will go over easier if you get ahold of yourself." Williams gave him time to calm down—as much as that was possible—and went on: "I'd like to take you to her, but I'm afraid you won't be as cooperative as you need to be at this point on your journey."

James took a deep breath. "I'm so tired of your bullshit. Say what you have to say."

Williams gestured for him to go first, and James stepped through the doorway. As they walked across an open space of the first floor of the building, the men in black kept a step behind James while Williams led the way.

"I miss the times when we were on good terms, James. In my past, that is. I'm thrilled for you to experience . . . well, you'll see." Before entering the next room, he said, "Restrain him."

James tried to wiggle, but the androids seized him, and one of them wrapped a gloved hand around his face, leaving him just enough space to suck in breaths through his nose. Shuffling his feet, he was led into the room. Even when James stopped resisting, they didn't let him be.

Lauren sat tied to a chair, her hands behind her back. She looked up at him with red eyes. A rogue strand of hair was stuck to her cheek. She said, "James, please, go. Run."

Williams cocked his head at her. "Can't run from this, Agent. You of all people should know."

One of the androids let James say, "I'm sorry, Lauren. Sorry I freaked out back there. Sorry I dragged you into this shit."

"You didn't," she replied, shaking her head. "Whatever he offers you, take it, but please leave."

"Not without you." He tried to step up to her, but a man in black pulled him back and didn't let go.

Williams circled the chair and put his hands on Lauren's shoulders, his white fingers long and bony. "I don't have much to offer, James. This is where this journey ends. This, here, is a courtesy. Say your goodbyes."

Lauren said, "You'll get through this, James. I know it."

Panicked, James looked at her, and then at the old man. There had to be a way out. "Just let us go."

Williams closed his eyes. "You know that can't happen. Because it hasn't happened, James."

The androids grabbed James's hands, and he was gagged once again.

Williams said, "Farewell doesn't do my dirty work as you've been led to believe. They're not killers, either. Well, not exclusively. Our original intention for it was, believe it or not, benevolent. We wanted to do good. We helped people escape difficult circumstances, hide, protect their loved ones. New lives, new identities . . ."

Lauren hung her head, too tired to keep it up. James saw her body tremble.

Williams threw a black hood on her head and continued, "In most cases, it's easy for people to disappear. One day they're around, the next they're not. Vanished who knows where. But sometimes, it needs to be more . . . final, unquestionable. There needs to be a body. Such is the case, I'm sorry to say, with Agent Farewell. That is, Casey Farewell. Take her," he ordered, and a man stepped into the room.

James's legs gave, and he would've dropped to the floor had the androids not been holding him upright. Frankie Mason, young and determined, stepped up to Lauren in three hard strides and pulled her to her feet. Up close, James saw a young man with something to prove. A man he recognized as his father and didn't recognize at all. His movements radiated with the harsh, brutish energy of an enforcer. His face, meanwhile, showed no sympathy for the captured woman.

"Do I want to know?" Frankie asked, eyeing the young woman whose arm he was gripping.

"No," Williams replied and, after Frankie gave him a nod, added, "Take good care of her."

Frankie Mason smirked. James shut his eyes for a moment, and when he opened them, he met Lauren's. As she was being dragged away, she whimpered, "Keep moving forward, okay?"

James grunted, but his mouth was clenched in the android's hand so tight it hurt. A moment later, the two disappeared, and Williams stepped up to him. "And this is it, James. Now you know the full story, don't you? Come, it's time for you to be on your way."

The robots dragged him across the main space, James's shoes leaving wiggly lines on the dirty concrete floor. The flying saucer, completely visible, sat where he'd left it, with its ramp lowered, familiar white light creeping out. The robots dropped him onto it, and he sat up, weakly supporting himself on one elbow. He brushed back his hair as Williams watched.

"I'd like to tell you that the hardest part is over, James, but that would be a lie. Living with it, with the cursed knowledge, that will be your true test."

"You've taken everything from me," James whispered in a small, hoarse voice.

Williams nodded. "Then we are even."

"What about Tom? You promised . . ." James would have laughed, if he had the strength to.

William's brow jerked up. "I'm afraid this machine only goes one way, James. But I will let you go with this. Your mother's name, Casey, as in *K. C.* Her middle name is Claire. What's her first name?"

"Fuck off," James mumbled, and he crawled up the ramp. It closed behind him. He made his way below deck to his bed, and before he passed out, he said, "Initiate the jump, Maggie. Please."

CHAPTER 26

———

He stirred awake sometime later, sweaty and sore all over with a cold nose and feet. Getting out of bed was a monumental task, and James dreaded it, instead turning on the thin mattress, wrapped in the sheets. His body trembled.

"Can you turn the heat up," he mumbled.

"Your vital signs indicate dehydration, James," the time machine replied. "I suggest a warm shower and a few glasses of water."

It did sound nice. The last time he'd consumed anything was the bitter coffee Lauren had offered, back in Toulouse. Yesterday? Two days ago? It was anyone's guess. He couldn't tell anything anymore. The past had become an elusive concept, lost somewhere between the moon and San Francisco, or wherever he was. Events of the last few days—*decades, almost*—replayed in his mind like bizarre dreams. Men in black, French super spies, Williams . . . and K. C. Farewell. *What's her first name?*

"Warm up that shower," James said, and he made himself tear the sheets off his body and set his feet on the cold floor.

Twenty minutes later, somewhat refreshed though still tired, he put on a fresh set of clothes and made himself coffee and a snack of dried fruits and yogurt. They didn't talk for hours as he paced the deck of the flying saucer, its walls smooth and solid. He tried to get some more sleep, drink some water. Where was he? Back on the moon, maybe, in the military base part of Peary-I. Back in the beginning, before the crash, whatever paradox that might create. Provided a word of Williams's had been true, which was a big *if*.

Finally, curiosity got the better of him, and James put on a jacket and headed outside. Light blinded him as he stepped off the ramp and onto gray sand, and the salty coolness of the ocean hit his nostrils with a gentle breeze. In the distance, water splashed and foamed, crashing against a familiar rock formation that had always looked to him like letters when he was a kid. He'd imagine they were the initials of some giant who'd lost them a long time ago, and there they remained, slowly being smoothed out by the ocean.

He walked along the beach on the narrow strip of wet sand, threatened by the cold water, hands in his pockets, shoulders hunched against the wind. When was this? He couldn't say, but ahead he spotted the oceanside bungalow he'd grown up in—a tiny one-story wooden hut painted blue and white, with a ring buoy on the wall by the door and floor-to-ceiling windows on the veranda. There was the old canoe rack that never held any canoes, and behind the house, he'd most certainly find the patio with a small stone fireplace. The beach was empty of people, and James approached the hut as if returning home. It seemed smaller than he'd remembered, more *observable*, hiding nothing from his sight. Unremarkable, almost.

He never considered knocking. Instead, he approached those large veranda windows and stood by them, just out of sight. In the living room, by the fire, Frankie Mason sat cross-legged on a colorful rug, guitar in his lap, as his mother nursed the newborn James.

"*K* for Katherine," James whispered.

His mother, young and beautiful, held him in her hands and smiled at Frankie as he strummed the guitar, and then she sang a song in a voice he thought he remembered. His mother, not yet Ekaterina Fortepianova, and his father, scruffy and long-haired and happy. One perfect moment captured between the past and the future, whatever that entailed for those three.

James listened for a few more minutes, humming along, and then he walked away, back to the flying saucer time machine, with its secret routes and missions, leaving this past well alone. *Keep moving forward,* Lauren had told him, and maybe that was the only thing left to do.

"Hey, Magpie, initiate the next jump."

ACKNOWLEDGMENTS

___

The journey of *Crescent Earth* has only just begun, and it's a journey more than a decade in the making. It started off circa 2009, when I was doodling in my tenth-grade notebook. At the time, it was a story about a scientist building a time machine on the moon, out of, of course, a car (Audi R8, I think). The gist of the story stuck, and I never stopped adding to it throughout the years since.

Speaking of influences, I really should credit some of the master storytellers who inspired this book. Time travel writers and filmmakers: Jack Finney, Stephen King, Terry Gilliam, Charlie Kaufman (not time travel per se, I know), Robert Zemeckis, and, honestly, too many others to name here. You know them, you get it. I could write a whole book just about time travel stories I've seen and read, but I'd like to keep it more personal here.

Huge thanks to my parents. To my dad, Anton, who showed me so many great and sad movies when I was probably too young to see them. To my mom, Zhanna, who is always in my corner, no matter what.

To my soul mate, Valerie, who's been my constant inspiration since high school, not just in writing but in life. To the many wonderful friends who helped me along the way, especially Sean Mullen, who listened to me ramble about this story for years. You are all amazing, and this book is yours.

A special thanks to my wonderful editors, David Grandouiller and Alan Zatkow, who helped me straighten out my thoughts and arrange them in a way that resulted in a narrative. They were way too nice about it, too.

Finally, I have to thank everyone who preordered a copy. Thank you for having trust and patience! Here you are:

Jonathan Allarie, Cass Lauer, Valeria Guryeva, Fabienne Jacquet, Zhanna Kamaeva, Valentina Kamaeva, Leah Bader, Travis Czap, Demitrius Covington, Vadim Korostiev-Rykov, Ryan Cummins, Britta Lindemulder, Sidney Williams, Jivika Rajani, Matt Maldonado, Kathryn Calamia, Arvind Nagarajan, Uttara Shekar, Samuel Philpot, Ashley Cavuto, Dmitry Novikov, Rose Afriyie, Josh Collier, Katrina Green, Patricia Giramma, Marina Gureva, Karina Nazhmudinova, Maria Fernanda Suarez Escalante, Samuel Taliaferro, Jordan Waterwash, Begona Pino, Michael Tener, Daniel Corey, Taz Lake, Joe Walters, Scott Wilke, Calvin Warden II, Kristofor Harris, Joshua Begley, Christopher Ramsey, Patty Arroyo, Omar Morales, Chad Coup, Daniel Prim, Valentin Polyakov, Jill Laing, Wes Locher, ChandaElaine Spurlock, Eric Koester, Sean Mullen, Anton Epifanov

Thank you all once again! See you in the next one!